Delfino's Journey

Delfino's Journey

Jo Harper

Texas Tech University Press

This book was set in Garamond and Casa Blanca Antique. The paper used in this book meets the minimum requirements of ANSI/NISO Z39.48-1992 (R1997).∞

Printed in the United States of America

Art and design by Bryce Burton

Library of Congress Cataloging-in-Publication Data
Harper, Jo.
Delfino's journey / by Jo Harper.
p. cm.
Summary: Delfino and his cousin Salvador leave their Aztec village in Mexico to search for work in the United States, where they endure dangerous and brutal conditions before ultimately finding success beyond all their dreams. Includes related explanatory notes and bibliography.
ISBN 0-89672-437-9 (book) — ISBN 0-89672-442-5 (teacher's supplement) [1. Illegal aliens—Fiction. 2. Mexicans—United States—Fiction. 3. Aztecs—Fiction. 4. Indians of Mexico--Fiction. 5. Cousins—Fiction. 6. Texas—Fiction.] I. Title.
PZ7.H23135 De 2000
[Fic]--dc21

00-010157

01 02 03 04 05 06 07 08 09 / 9 8 7 6 5 4 3 2 1

Texas Tech University Press
Box 41037
Lubbock, Texas 79409-1037 USA

1-800-832-4042
ttup@ttu.edu
http://www.ttup.ttu.edu

Acknowledgments

Many people helped in the creation and publication of this book. Joan Lowery Nixon gave the first word of encouragement when the manuscript was only two paragraphs long. Without that word, the novel would never have been begun. Jorge Julian from Ahuelican, Mexico inspired the story and contributed invaluable personal information. My daughter Josephine gave plot suggestions and cracked the whip. Her contribution was beyond the call of daughterhood. My son Jim provided real world details his bookish mother would never have thought of. My daughter De Aaon, an exacting proofreader, read and printed in spite of her busy schedule. My writing buddies Molly Anderegg, Bobbie Wolfe, and Therese Griffiths provided critiques and encouragement over a period of years. My friend Renée Cho made valuable suggestions; my friend Dr. D. W. Gunn contributed his insights; and my friend Jere Pfister loyally pitched in. Judith Keeling, the most amiable of editors, is due enormous credit for the careful production of *Delfino's Journey.* Jackie McLean did yeoman's work in her careful reading of the book and in writing the teacher's supplement. Bryce Burton, amazingly, did the illustrations exactly as I wanted them. Long hours and close deadlines did not dampen the Texas Tech team's enthusiasm, and the project was fun to the end. To all, my thanks and gratitude.

Dedication

For Josephine and Judith

Contents

1

The Crossing

"We're sinking!" Delfino exclaimed. Rio Grande water was rising in the old, wooden boat. Delfino felt it creep up his shoes. He saw a faint glimmer where a few pale stars reflected in the water gathered in the bottom.

The *coyote*[1] guide swore in the darkness, cursing the depth of the water and the heavy rains far upstream.

Could he still get them across the river and into Texas? Delfino wondered. He had heard that some years the water was so low a person could walk across. Not this year. Not his luck.

The summer night was warm. A thin moon slipped from behind a cloud, and a ray of light struck the *coyote*'s gold tooth. Delfino shivered with a sudden chill.

"Can you boys swim?"

What a question! Boys from inland Aztec villages in the south of Mexico didn't swim.

Delfino looked toward Salvador. His cousin's big body was a motionless, hunched shadow. Never had he felt more impatient with his cousin's slow wits. But it was his impatience that had gotten them into this mess.

Salvador had wanted to wait for Bernardo, the *coyote* from their own village. He would have crossed far downriver near Nuevo Laredo.

"I don't like this man," Salvador had said, speaking in their native Nahuatl. "I don't like the way he makes me feel." But Delfino wouldn't listen. He was in a hurry and gave almost all his money to the strange *coyote* who said he would take them across at a deserted spot. Delfino had knotted his knife, along with the few pesos he had left, into a handkerchief and put it deep in the pocket of his baggy pants.

The *coyote,* crouched on his knees, scooped up water and tossed it over the side of the boat, swearing. Delfino worked beside him. He saw that they were getting nowhere. He scooped faster and faster.

Salvador sat still, his shadowy hand making the sign of the cross.

"Help us, Cousin," Delfino said.

Obediently, Salvador began to scoop water with his hands.

"This boat's going down," the *coyote* said. He staggered forward. "You'll have to get to San Antonio on your own."

"I paid you! Give me back my money!"

The *coyote* brushed away the demand. "I'm gone."

Desperate, Delfino jumped on the *coyote* and pummeled him. They fell, splashing into the water gathered in the boat.

The *coyote* grabbed Delfino's hair and cracked his head against the side of the boat. He kicked, driving his foot like a locomotive into Delfino's stomach. Then he lunged over the side and was gone, Delfino's money still in his pocket.

Delfino's heart dropped to the bottom of his aching stomach, and he felt a new pang—fear. He and Salvador were alone in a sinking boat in the middle of the Rio Grande. His thin shoulders shuddered as he felt water rising. He struggled to his feet and grabbed Salvador's hand. "Jump, Cousin!"

They plunged into the water. Then he found the edge of the sinking boat and clung to it, frightened and shocked. Salvador clung beside him. Their weight dipped the boat toward them.

I've got to figure something out, Delfino thought. There has to be some way out of this mess.

Maybe we could turn the boat over. Then it wouldn't sink. Air would hold it up. "Lift . . . lift the boat. Turn it over," he told Salvador. "One . . . two . . . three . . . "

They tried to heave the boat upward. Delfino knew that Salvador was strong. His big arms could hoist more than twice as much as Delfino's small, skinny ones, more than any man's in their village . . . but with nothing to brace their feet on, there was no way to lift.

Delfino and Salvador clung to the boat, but Delfino knew it would go down soon.

There has to be a way, he thought.

He felt the water around him. He wiggled his lean body and kicked. The boat moved down, then up. He pushed with his hands, then released. The boat went up and down again.

"Cousin, maybe we can rock it over!" Delfino exclaimed.

Hand over hand, he pulled himself to the opposite side. Then they began to rock the boat. Down, up . . . down, up . . . . They moved slowly at first. Then, finding their rhythm, they began to go faster and faster. Each time they rocked the boat, it rose higher in the air. It was working!

Delfino gulped a deep breath. "Okay, Salvador. Flip it over!"

He let go so Salvador could flip the boat. He kicked hard, hoping to stay afloat a few seconds. He heard a splat, and Salvador called softly, "We did it!"

Then, kicking and flailing, Delfino went under. Down . . . down . . . water rushing in his ears . . . darkness everywhere, his slight hundred pounds of weight pulling him deeper and deeper . . .

His lungs hurt. If only it weren't so dark. If only he could see. Where was he? He kicked wildly and bumped against Salvador's leg.

Salvador's strong hand grabbed his arm and pulled him upward. Delfino hit the surface. He gasped the warm, sweet summer air . . . then he slipped from his cousin's grip and went down again. Water burned his nose and roared in his ears. He fought with all his strength.

He struggled, rose, and knew he was going to sink again. He grabbed uselessly at the surface as if it were something solid.

Take it easy, he told himself. Calm down. If you are going to die in the lonely darkness of the Rio Grande, you might as well do it like a man.

Delfino knew that death by drowning was a good death. His grandfather had told him about the special heaven for those who die a watery death. The rain god, Tlaloc, and his wife, Chalchihuitlicue, Lady Precious Green, rule that heaven. Delfino knew it was a happy kingdom of green plants, bright rainbows, and dancing butterflies.[2] But he did not want to go to heaven, not even to one of the best of the seven Aztec lands of the dead. He wanted to live.

I'm not going to die yet. I'm going to stay right here on this earth. I will not drown!

He began to move his arms and legs in rhythm. He paddled rapidly, eagerly gulping air. It soothed his aching lungs. Strength flooded through his body as he moved through the water. He had it figured out. He could swim!

He felt a moment's exultation. But Delfino couldn't see anything except the water's dark surface. Where was Salvador? Which way should he swim? Was he moving in a circle?

The moon! Lady Golden Bells! Delfino thought. The pale arc of the waning moon had been on his left. Hoping the clouds hadn't covered it, Delfino looked up, paddling hard. Like a curved blade, it shone coldly in the dark sky. If he could just keep it to his left, he could make it across the river. Lady Golden Bells would lead him.[3]

"Salvador!" he shouted. "Salvador! Salvador!" He knew he might be heard by the Border Patrol, but he had to find his cousin. "Salvador!"

"Here. I am here." Salvador's voice came to him across the water.

Delfino paddled toward the sound. A dim shape floated toward him. It was the overturned boat, held up by air trapped inside. Salvador was pushing it.

Delfino caught hold gratefully.

The current carried the boys downstream, but they stayed afloat and kept the moon to the left.

Why did I ever leave my village? Delfino asked himself. But he knew why. He remembered the pain he had known in that dusty, loveless place.

Grandfather had died. When his sister Teresa had married, her husband, Melchor, had taken her to live in his own village to please his conservative parents. The others in the family were all cruel. Except Salvador. Salvador had shared his food. Salvador had stood by him.

Delfino's *tonali*—his fate—hadn't been good so far, but he wouldn't accept that he was destined to have a bad *tonali*. Across the border in Texas lay a destiny he could shape for himself.[4] He would make money for Teresa and loyal Salvador would help him. They always stuck together.

Delfino's wet clothes and shoes dragged at him. They were heavy. He longed to take them off, but he knew he couldn't.

I'd arrive naked as a newborn in the new land, he thought.

Angry, he kicked harder. It made him mad to think he got into this mess because of his own stupidity. He was always in too much of a hurry. Even Salvador had known they should wait, not go with a strange, scowling, gold-toothed *coyote*.

The murky darkness lightened, and the boys, kicking and clinging to the overturned boat, could see the riverbank. It lay very near. They kicked harder, guiding the boat ahead of them. In the silent dawn, there was no sound except water sloshing as they moved.

Delfino's heart pounded. He and Salvador were lost and alone, but before them lay the Promised Land.

Soon they were wading out of the river. They had made it.

2

The Promised Land

Delfino and Salvador dragged their tired bodies onto the sandy bank. Delfino felt like leaving the boat in the river. Let the thing go, he thought. But he was dragging the boat out even as the thought came. Maybe they would need kindling. Or a board for protection.

The boys sank, exhausted, on the sand. Delfino knew what it was like to be tired—tired from working too long on too little food and tired from lifting too much. But this was different. He had never felt like this before. This tiredness was a slow, mellow ache that soaked through his body.

Dawn was rapidly becoming bright day. Delfino knew that they must get away from the river. The Border Patrol could find them there too easily. But his eyes would not stay open. He slept.

When he awoke, the sun was bright overhead. Hot and thirsty, he sat up, rubbed his eyes and ran his hands through his hair. It felt stiff and crusty. Salvador was kneeling at the edge of the water, splashing his face. His Virgin of Guadalupe[1] card was lying on a rock drying in the sun.

Delfino felt in his pocket. The handkerchief with his knife and pesos in it was gone! He struck the palm of one hand with an angry fist. Never mind the money. It was only a few pesos. But he needed that knife. He looked around at the ground where he had slept. But he knew it wasn't there. It was long gone in the Rio Grande.

Wouldn't you know that what they needed was lost to the river, and the Virgin of Guadalupe was saved? Delfino had a particular disdain for that Virgin because he saw her worship as a sellout. Hadn't she appeared at the site of the goddess Coatlicue's shrine? Hadn't she spoken Nahuatl?

What's the matter with me? he thought. Why am I thinking about that junk, as if I believed in the goddess?—or as if I didn't have more important things to think about, like my sister Teresa.

Nothing was as important as getting money for Teresa. He had crossed the border because of her. She was expecting a child, her second. The first had died after a hard delivery, and Teresa had been so weak, Delfino had been afraid she would die, too. He wanted her to go to a real doctor and have this baby in a hospital. No one else in his family thought that was important. They thought everything was in the hands of fate.

The priest, Padre Ignacio, who visited their village every month, agreed with Delfino. But Teresa's young husband didn't have money for a doctor or hospital. Besides, he was old-fashioned and thought like the rest of the family. In his mind, not doctors but fate, *tonali*, determined what would happen. So it was up to Delfino to find the money for his sister. Teresa was only eighteen, and so small and thin that Delfino felt her life could snap as quickly as one of her birdlike bones.

Delfino sighed and looked across the river. The distance was short. Incredibly short. He could walk that far in ten minutes. An easy walk. Could run it in five. Yet they had been in the water a long time—a long time, kicking hard. Delfino wondered how far they had drifted.

He knew they must get away from the river before the Border Patrol came by. They must go north—away from Mexico and into the land of plenty.

As he looked around, Delfino saw no signs of plenty. Bare desert mountains loomed in the distance. Between the river and the mountains was scrub brush. And sand. And scattered cactus. "Just us and you, my spiny friends," Delfino said out loud. "We are stuck out in the sand together."

Now he had started talking to cactus. Besides the bad luck of being dumped by his *coyote,* he was going crazy, too.

"What, Cousin?" Salvador asked, looking at Delfino in his mild, good-natured way. As always, Salvador's gentle dark eyes seemed to be gazing somewhere else.

"I said we are stuck in the sand," Delfino answered, punching Salvador affectionately on the shoulder.

Salvador nodded. He walked over to a cactus, carefully picked off a spine, and signaled Delfino to come.

He wants to make the morning offering,[2] Delfino realized. The sun was high; it was late for the offering. Still, they had just awakened.

Delfino joined his cousin and carefully picked a cactus spine. Then, like Salvador, he jabbed each of his ear lobes with a quick thrust and caught a drop of blood on each forefinger. They raised their hands and cast the blood into the air.

"Take this small gift, Quetzalcoatl.[3] May it comfort you," Salvador said.

Delfino was glad Salvador had remembered the morning offering Grandfather had taught them—not only because it was good to honor Quetzalcoatl as they entered the new land, but also because it brought Grandfather to mind.

To remember Grandfather was like going into the restful shade of a sheltering tree. He had always been calm and gentle. He had nothing to do with fierce and bloody old Aztec ways. Or with drunkenness and anger. Grandfather had taught Salvador and Delfino to honor the peaceful ways of Quetzalcoatl, who wanted only fruit, flowers, or a drop of blood as an offering.

Delfino longed for the cool safety of night. "When it's dark we can go toward the lights. We can figure out where there's a town."

Salvador nodded. "We can wait under the scrub brush."

Delfino knew that daytime was their enemy, not only because they could be seen, but because the heat was a killer. Yet he itched to get moving. He had to start. Had to look for the promise in the Promised Land.

"Let's walk," he said.

Salvador rose, his broad, six-foot frame towering above Delfino. "Which way?" he asked agreeably.

Delfino gestured with his skinny arm. He signaled a direction away from the river—northeast . . . maybe. With the sun directly overhead, he couldn't be sure.

"Salvador, I lost the knife in the river," Delfino said. Then he gestured at the boat. "Let's take a board."

They braced their feet against the boat and jerked in unison. A plank broke loose. Delfino was glad. The board was their weapon. He carried it on his shoulder like a rifle as they set out, away from the river.

Their shadows were small dark spots beneath their feet. They walked awkwardly, their shoes stiff and still damp. Even their clothes were stiff and hardened.

Hunger gnawed Delfino's belly. It seemed a long time since the hasty tortillas he and Salvador had eaten the afternoon before. Now they didn't have any money for food, even if there were a place to spend it.

Delfino wished they could meet the other guide, the one the *coyote* said would take them to San Antonio. But they wouldn't know him if they saw him. Besides, they had drifted far downstream.

Delfino's stiff body loosened as he walked. Even his shoes softened. He and Salvador now swung along smoothly. Delfino's spirits lifted.

We are leaving the bad old days behind, he thought.

He was leaving a drunken father who beat him . . . a powerless mother, endlessly shouting at the younger children . . . an old crone of a grandmother who wouldn't turn loose of a peso or a crumb . . . those were part of the bad old days that drove Delfino from the village. After Teresa married and moved away, Delfino went all the way to Mexico City to escape his house and to make money. But he couldn't earn much—

certainly not as much as he needed for Teresa now. So he was trying Texas, and his heart was full of hope.

Good days lie ahead, he told himself, happy ones, as bright as that sun. He walked faster. He felt a little thirsty.

In a few hours, thirst became a torment. Could they turn back to the river? No. They had gone too far. Better to press on. Keep going.

If they could eat the cactus fruit, the prickly pears, they would feel better. But the prickly pears, like the cactus they grew on, were covered with fine needles. Needles that could kill. Delfino had seen what happened when cattle ate the cactus. The thin spines in their mouths and intestines tortured them until they died—a slow, agonizing death.

Delfino's dry lips hurt. They were cracked from the heat. But he couldn't moisten them. His tongue lay in his mouth like a dry stick.

I could burn the spines off a prickly pear if only I had a match, Delfino thought. He remembered how he used to burn them back in Ahuelican. Then the cattle ate the thick green leaves safely, and he ate the fruit. Inside the thick skin, it was purple and sweet like a giant grape.

Delfino's mouth contracted at the memory. His belly knotted with longing.

The board was heavy. Delfino threw it away with an angry gesture. Salvador walked to where the board lay, his big shoulders hunched. "I'll carry it," he said. His voice, now thick and raspy, blurred the crisp, clear Nahuatl sounds.

Delfino felt weak. The heat weighed him down. It leached the strength out of him. He staggered. Then he felt Salvador's big hand on his elbow, steadying him. He remembered the corn he used to raise in their village, Ahuelican. It grew, green and straight until the summer sun began to blaze. When that happened, the corn shriveled and turned brown even though Delfino broke his back carrying water. When the sun became a fierce torch, the corn died.

I am like that corn.

But the corn always grows again. The Corn God rises although his head is cut off.

Suddenly, a lake glistened in the distance. Delfino ran toward the cool blue water. He would drink. The first sip would fall in his parched mouth like a tear onto desert sand. But he would drink more. There was plenty to quench his drought. He would swallow quick gulps until he was satisfied. Then he would plunge in. The lake would cool him. It would soothe his burning skin.

The lake disappeared.

Delfino stopped, then ran again, slipping and stumbling as he went.

Hold on, he told himself. That's a mirage. Take it easy. Stop acting like a child.

Delfino turned and saw Salvador staring after him. "Cousin, I'm running *loco* for water," Delfino called. "Let's take a chance and eat some prickly pears."

Salvador nodded, his soft eyes vague as always. Together they walked to one of the scattered cactus. A small snake lay beside it, sunning himself.

"Good day to you, Coatzintli," Salvador said, addressing the snake courteously. "Now we will have good luck," he said to Delfino. "Coatzintli will bring it to us."

He nudged a ripe pear to the ground with the board. Then he nudged two more off—green ones.

"Can we break off some of the board for a knife?" Delfino wondered aloud. But he knew that was impossible. They had taken a good strong plank. The sides were firm and hard.

"Maybe chew a piece off," Salvador suggested.

Delfino shook his head. "It would take too long. I'll smash the pear."

He took the board and gouged the fruit hard with the corner. It slipped. He tried again. The thick skin broke. Purple liquid stained the sand. Most of it was lost, but Delfino thrust his fingers into the small fruit and pulled out a bit of seedy meat. It fell in the sandy burrow of his mouth like a drop of sweet rain. Salvador broke the pear open wider. The shell was soon empty.

Delfino knew if they looked long enough they could find another ripe prickly pear. But he couldn't wait. He forced open the green ones. He and Salvador pulled out the pale, paperlike pulp. Salvador slowly brushed off each small bite and looked at it carefully before he put it in his mouth. Delfino put his in quickly and chewed greedily. The green fruit was bitter. He didn't care; it was moist. He didn't even care about the fine spines he felt in his tongue.

He looked across at big Salvador hunched down on one knee. Salvador had the same round head, round face, and straight black hair as the other men from their village. But he stretched skyward above everyone else. And his black, almond-shaped eyes were different—different because of their mild, vague expression. He always seemed to be gazing toward some distant land no one else could see. That's why in Ahuelican they had called Salvador *el raro,* "the strange one."

Delfino felt his strength returning. His eyes scanned the horizon. He saw movement.

"Cousin," he said in a soft, excited voice, "we're not lost any more. There's a highway over there!"

3

A Free Ride

A bright reflection floated smoothly and steadily above the sand in the distance. Delfino knew it was a car.

"We'll follow that road, Cousin," he said, pointing toward the reflection. He spoke softly, not wanting to waste his strength.

Salvador nodded and rose from his crouched position. Purple juice from the prickly pear had stained his mouth. Drops of sweat clustered on his forehead and rolled down his face in little streams. He wiped his mild, vague eyes with the back of his hand and nodded agreeably.

The boys did not hurry as they walked. There was a road to follow. It must lead somewhere. It would surely lead to water.

Now that several hours had passed, Delfino could tell that they were going east because their shadows lay before them. Salvador carried his thick shoulders hunched and his arms rounded at his sides. He cast a broad shadow. Delfino thought it looked like a giant desert turtle, its head just peeping out of its shell. His own shadow beside it looked thin and brittle with grasshopper legs.

As they neared the highway, they saw it stretching before them like another river, bright with the sun. I hope we don't have so much trouble crossing this one, Delfino thought wryly.

No cars were in sight now, and waves of heat rose dizzily from the pavement. The boys stayed a little distance from the highway as they followed it. There was no place to conceal themselves in the level expanse, but they felt less noticeable away from the road.

A pair of yellow butterflies rose from a cactus blossom and fluttered around them. Then, brightly dancing in the air, they flew away.

Salvador smiled. He looked as innocently joyful as a child. "The happy dead[1] have come to encourage us," he said.

Delfino nodded. Grandfather had taught them that butterflies were souls, come back from the dead to visit their families. Much as he still respected Grandfather, Delfino now doubted the old beliefs. Just the same, seeing the bright creatures and remembering Grandfather lightened his heart, and he smiled back at Salvador.

They began counting the cars to entertain themselves, talking a little in spite of their dry, wooden tongues.

"Ten," Salvador said as a white pickup truck came into view.

"They sure must like trucks around here," Delfino commented.

Of the nine vehicles that had whizzed by, six had been pickup trucks. But this one was not going fast. It was a white pickup with a gun rack in the back window. It stopped. A man in a cowboy hat got out.

"Oh, no," Delfino whispered. "This may be the Border Patrol. Get ready to run."

Pushing his hat to the back of his head, the man called to the boys in Spanish, "Do you want to work? I'm a farmer. I'm not the police. I'm not with the Border Patrol."

Delfino turned to face the man. From the corner of his eye, he saw Salvador's turtlelike shadow moving awkwardly away. There was fear in the movement.

Tucking your head in your turtle shell won't keep you safe, Delfino thought. Aloud he said, "Don't be afraid, Cousin. He says he's not the Border Patrol. We have to take a chance. Let's talk to the man."

Delfino started toward the pickup. Salvador followed three steps behind. As Delfino got closer, he saw that the pickup had a small dent and a red smudge on the right fender.

The man was big—bigger than Salvador. His square jaw was softened by jowls, and he had a large, meaty nose. His blue eyes were the palest Delfino had ever seen. He wore high-heeled boots and a big silver belt buckle that shone from under his hanging belly.

"You boys look like you'd know what to do with a good meal," he said in a friendly voice, still speaking Spanish. "I could use a couple more hands. Hoe cotton. Move some rocks. I'm headed away from the border."

"Where is your *rancho?"* Delfino asked.

"North. Far from the border."

Delfino tried not to stare at the large lump that kept moving in the man's jaw. The man turned his head and spat brown juice onto the ground.

The sun gleamed on the dark brown liquid. Revolted, Delfino turned his eyes away. Speaking rapid Nahuatl, he told Salvador what the man had said. Salvador knew only a few words of Spanish. He had not left their Aztec village and worked in Mexico City, as Delfino had.

"Injuns, huh," the man muttered.

Salvador was staring at the American as Delfino talked. His mild, distant eyes did not change expression even when he shifted them to Delfino. "I don't feel good with this man. I'd rather walk. We'll find another man."

Delfino was annoyed. "You act like jobs and rides come along every hour. We don't know where to go or what to do. We've got to have food. And water. We have to go with this man."

Delfino's mouth ached as he said the word *water*. He looked at the *gringo.* "We are going with you." He spoke with decision, but his stomach tightened into a nervous knot.

The man's pale eyes narrowed. The puffy skin around them lifted with his smile, making him look more grotesque than friendly. He opened the door of the truck and raised the lid on a chest behind the seat. "How about a little drink?"

The chest was full of ice, and the water the *gringo* poured in white cups was cold. Delfino's trembling hands felt its chill as he raised the drink. He swallowed in rapid gulps. His eyes hurt from the cold and tears came to them. Ashamed, he looked at the ground as he handed back his cup and said, "Shall we get in the back?"

The man turned his head and again spat brown liquid. "Naw. You boys get right up in the cab. Get yourselves out of the sun."

"Come on," Delfino said to Salvador. He led the way to the other side of the truck and got in first. Wanting to please as always, Salvador followed, his movements uneasy.

The slow turtle, thought Delfino. And look at me now, wedged in between these big guys like a sliver of cheese between two fat rolls. He smiled at the thought. He didn't care if he was wedged in . . . he was riding . . . he was going far from the border . . . he had a job.

But an uneasy sense of doubt nagged him. Salvador's feelings about the *coyote* had been right. Maybe he was right about this man, too.

The air in the truck was cool. The seats were soft. Delfino brushed his doubts away and settled into the comfort. Sitting in the high pickup cab and speeding down the highway made him feel powerful. He hadn't known a sense of power many times in his life, but he couldn't stay awake to enjoy it. Lulled by the hum of the motor and soothed by the cool air, he crossed the border into sleep and began to dream.

In his dream, he was on a street in Mexico. A street vendor in a big sombrero was selling roasting ears. Delfino's mouth watered as he smelled the sweet aroma of cooked grain. His stomach leaped in anticipation as the vendor brushed the yellow corn with red *chili.* Delfino reached for the roasting ear. The vendor peered at him from under his sombrero. He had a pasty, *gringo* face and pale eyes. His fat mouth, circled in brown, laughed horribly.

Delfino turned away. Fragrant steam rose from the corn and warmed his face. He opened his mouth for the first sweet bite.

Before his teeth reached the corn, he saw a dog walking toward him. The street was now strangely deserted. The dog was the color of red clay, with short legs and fat sides that stood out from its body and shook as it walked. It waddled up to Delfino and looked at him with pleading eyes.[2]

Delfino reached down and gave the dog his corn. The animal crunched the roasting ear, grain and cob together. Then the dog began to change. Its smooth red coat turned scraggly and stuck out in angry bristles. It grew long and lean, like a huge coyote. Its eyes shone yellow, and it growled.

Delfino turned and ran down the empty street. Sweat covered his body, but his heart was cold with fear. The street before him widened and became a desert, dotted with cactus.

The coyote chased him, coming closer and closer, snarling and snapping. Its hot breath was dry. It scorched Delfino's skin. He ran harder, his legs pumping frantically and his lungs bursting. But the great coyote stayed close behind.

Pain stabbed Delfino's leg as the animal's teeth sunk in. Panting and sobbing, he turned and pounded the coyote with his fists. But the coyote held fast, growling. With one hand, Delfino grabbed a handful of the beast's hair. He jabbed at its yellow eyes with the other. The coyote let go and shrank back, snarling. Red blood flowed down Delfino's leg. The coyote leaped at his throat. Delfino raised his arms to shield his face and fell backwards onto the ground. He could see nothing but that snarl. In the coyote's bloody mouth, a gold tooth gleamed.

Salvador's voice came to him. "Cousin, wake up. You are dreaming."

For a moment, Delfino couldn't think where he was. He turned to his left. Pale, knowing eyes looked down at him. Delfino shivered.

The big American at the steering wheel said, "I guess you boys could do with a meal."

Delfino saw that they were in a village. They parked at a place with yellow arches. Outside the building, the sun beat down onto the bright yellow tables.

They went inside. Delfino had never eaten in a restaurant. He carried dry, crackerlike tortillas for his meals when he was away from home.

Inside the restaurant, the odor of frying meat made him weak with longing. The bright sun shone through wide windows and reflected off more yellow tables and off yellow tile. Delfino was dazzled and confused.

A young girl behind the counter spoke to him in Spanish. "What will you have?"

Delfino shook his head, not knowing what to say.

The big American said something in English to the girl, who filled a tray with food in paper containers. At the table, Delfino picked up a fat, hot sandwich and took a bite. Warm cheese and tangy tomato sauce spurted into his mouth. He noticed, surprised, that all his fried potatoes were exactly the same size and the same even, golden color. He stuffed them greedily in his mouth. He thought he had never had so wonderful a meal.

Heaving a relaxed sigh, Delfino looked at the people in the restaurant. None of them were thin. As he drank the thick sweet drink, he looked out the window at the people on the street. None of them were ragged.

Delfino was sure he had been right to come with this man. Soon he would have money to send to Teresa. She could go to a real doctor. She could have milk to drink and meat to eat. This was the Promised Land. They were lucky.

4

The Farm

A man entered the restaurant just as they were leaving. He was dressed almost like the American they were with—cowboy hat, boots, and a silver belt buckle. He was older, though, but lean and strong-looking. Delfino noticed that deep wrinkles slanted upward from the corners of his eyes, as if he had spent his whole life smiling. He wasn't smiling now. He was looking at them thoughtfully.

"Mornin', Buck," the American they were with said, as he touched the brim of his hat and walked past without pausing, his eyes straight ahead. When they got to the pickup, he spat a long brown stream on the sidewalk. Delfino felt his stomach turn; he was afraid he would lose his meal. He climbed in the truck quickly, closed his eyes, and took a deep breath.

They drove long miles. At last, Delfino broke the silence. "*Señor*, what do they call you?"

From under his cowboy hat, the American's pale blue eyes peered down at him. "*El patrón*. The boss. They call me Boss."

Boss pulled a dark square of tobacco from his shirt pocket and took a bite. His large, soft mouth, edged in brown, spread into a smile. "Farm's right over there."

Delfino sat up tall between Boss and Salvador. This was his first job in the land of plenty. His heart beat with excitement.

No other cars rolled down the dusty dirt road. No houses stood against the horizon. But the mesquite, scrub brush, and expanse of grass became fields with long, even rows.

They stopped. A tall fence bordered the *rancho*. There were a couple of small buildings outside it and two larger ones inside. Delfino could see that there was also an animal pen. Boss stepped out of the pickup and opened the gate. The fence looked strange to Delfino. It was metal. And on top were four thin wires. When they drove through, Boss got out again and closed the gate carefully.

He took them to one of the buildings—a long unpainted wooden one with a porchlike shelter attached. "You'll stay here in the bunkhouse. The rest of the men are working. Go on in. Make yourselves to home." And he left.

In the bunkhouse, rows of cots, each with a blanket, stood against flatboard walls. There were fifteen of them. Through the back window, Delfino saw an outhouse.

"Not bad, eh, Cousin?" he said amiably as he sat down on a cot. "After sitting all day, I still feel tired. A real lazybones, huh? Why don't we rest a few minutes, then we can look around the farm." Delfino gestured toward another cot as he spoke.

Salvador shook his head. "I'll sit on the floor."

Delfino lay down. Salvador just didn't know how to enjoy life, and Delfino couldn't help him with that. He closed his eyes and stretched comfortably. Here he was in the Promised Land, and he had a job. Soon all his dreams would come true. He would have money for Teresa and some for himself, too.

He imagined himself walking down an American street dressed in tight jeans and a bright blue shirt. He wore a straw cowboy hat. It perched on his head at an angle. A soft-eyed girl with a heart-shaped face looked at him admiringly. He swaggered past her, pretending not to notice her adoring eyes.

Lost in his fantasy, Delfino dozed.

Suddenly, he felt himself dragged to his feet. A thick-bodied, heavy-faced man held him roughly by the shirt.

"Pig! Runt!" he growled in Spanish.

Before Delfino could speak, the man hit him in the jaw. Pain jarred through all the bones in his face.

"What did I do wrong?"

Again, the man's broad fist cut through the air. It crashed into Delfino's face.

Voices spoke in Spanish. Dimly, Delfino saw a group of men gathering.

"Stop!"

"Leave the boy alone."

"Let him go, Lázaro."

The heavy hand, still grasping Delfino's chest, shoved him back.

Delfino staggered and fell. A heavy boot rushed toward him. Delfino squeezed his eyes closed, rolled into a ball, gritted his teeth, and tensed for the blow.

Nothing happened.

Laughter sounded.

Delfino opened his eyes and saw the thick-bodied, hard-eyed man twisting and turning in Salvador's arms. The man spewed oaths, but Salvador, his face gentle and his eyes mild, held the brute fast. He was like a large teddy bear hugging a bull.

Someone slammed a door. The group of men scattered, muttering softly to each other.

"Lázaro met his match."

"The strong man met a stronger."

"*Sí.* A gentle lamb caught the wild bull."

Delfino looked at Lázaro's hate-filled face and glowering eyes. He knew the brute would strike again as soon as Salvador let him go.

"I don't know what we can do now, Cousin," Delfino said in Nahuatl. "This guy's as mean as sin."

Lázaro struggled and swore again.

Salvador twisted Lázaro to the floor, sat astride him, and pinned his arms down. "I can sit like this a long time," he said mildly.

Before anyone could ask what he had said, the door slammed again.

"It's Slick."

"Slick's here."

The man they called Slick was thin and stoop shouldered with a stubble of beard. He was carrying a rifle. Sunlight gleamed along the barrel.

"What's going on? You men ain't nothin' but a pack of trouble," he said in Spanish. He gestured with the rifle for Salvador to get up.

Salvador did, stepping back beside Delfino as Lázaro lumbered to his feet swearing.

"Okay, now, scatter," Slick said. "Scatter and settle down." He glanced at the men and gave Lázaro a meaningful stare.

Lázaro sat down on his bed and glowered.

Delfino noticed drops splattering on the floor. Red drops. Blood.

A small, weathered man touched his shoulder. "Your face is bleeding. Come with me." He led Delfino outside to a water spigot and turned it on. Delfino splashed his face. The shock of cold water cleared his head and stopped his bleeding.

"Who is this Lázaro? Why did he hit me?" Delfino asked in Spanish.

"Because you were on his bed. Nothing more. He does meanness for Slick because he gets cigarettes and whiskey. He does other meanness just to be mean. He torments us all, as if our lives weren't miserable enough."

Delfino stared at the man. Why are they miserable in the land of plenty? he wondered.

A bell sounded. Men filed out of the bunkhouse and went toward another building. The sullen Lázaro, his coarse face brutish, was among them. Slick followed.

The men did look miserable. They walked stiffly, as if their muscles ached and their feet were sore. Some of them wore crude sandals made of cut tires. All of them wore ragged clothes and had dull, hopeless faces.

"Get your friend. It's time to eat. Lázaro's okay for now," the thin man said.

Delfino tried to go back into the bunkhouse, but a steady stream of men crowding out the door held him back. When all the men were out, he went in. Salvador was crouched in the corner.

"Come, Cousin. We can eat now."

Salvador nodded, and got up.

They followed the men into a metal building. There were big sliding doors at each end of the single room, and there was a single window. The floor was dirt, and the dim bulb that hung from the ceiling seemed to cast more shadows than light. Shuffling men blended into the hot semidarkness. Delfino put his hand on Salvador's arm.

The warm, steamy odor of food filled the air. After a moment, Delfino's eyes grew used to the light. The men had formed a line. They picked up metal spoons and metal plates from a table, and a fat, greasy man wearing a dirty white apron dished out beans and rice. Men sat at long wooden tables, eating in silence.

Delfino and Salvador got in line. When their turn came, Delfino was surprised at how big the servings were. As he and Salvador sat down at a table, he saw that men were getting in line for second helpings, but a heavy sense of sadness—of hopelessness—lay over them.

A soft hum of voices began to rise from the tables. Delfino was glad to hear the men talking. The sound would cover his questions. Something seemed wrong. Bad wrong. He had to find out what.

"They seem to give plenty of food," he said hesitantly to the bony-faced man sitting beside him.

"There's always lots of beans and rice. Sometimes they give us melons, too, and bananas." The man looked up from his plate and smiled wryly.

"Then this is a good place?"

The man looked at him with narrowed eyes. "Don't you know where you are?"

Delfino shook his head.

"*Hombre,* this is a slave camp."[1]

Delfino put his spoon down. The room whirled. Weakness swept over him. Then nausea. He pushed his plate back.

His thoughts whirled faster than the room. This man is crazy. There aren't slaves anymore. Maybe he means they work terribly hard. Or maybe he is teasing me. That's it; he is joking.

But the man looked at Delfino frankly. His face showed compassion.

"The food . . . ?" Delfino could barely whisper.

The man laughed bitterly. "Yeah, there's food. Eat, work, sleep. That's it. That's our life. We're penned up like animals and guarded day and night."

Delfino looked at Salvador sitting beside him. He was hunched over the table, steadily spooning rice into his mouth. For the first time, Delfino was glad Salvador couldn't understand Spanish. He didn't know what a terrible place they had found on this side of the border. Maybe he wouldn't have to know. Delfino would figure something out.

"Doesn't anyone ever run away?" he asked the man softly.

"Sometimes they try. A couple have tried since they brought me here a year ago. One guy climbed the fence. Poor devil didn't understand about the electricity. He died on the hot wires. Another one ran from the field when we were working. That was dumb. Slick shot him."

"He didn't kill him, did he?" Delfino tried to keep the horror out of his voice.

"Sure he did. They don't want a guy who is sick or injured. Especially one who tried to escape. Slick shot him in the head."

5

Dogs from Hell

Delfino couldn't sleep that night. A few hours before, to have a cot of his own had seemed like a luxury. Now it only seemed like part of the trap he was caught in. He lay on his back, his hands behind his head, staring at nothing. Eleven other men were in the room. Two cots were empty, and Delfino and Salvador had left the empty ones between themselves and the other men. After the problem with Lázaro, they wanted to sleep as far away from the others as possible.

Salvador was resting peacefully, unaware of the trouble they were in. Delfino could hear his deep, regular breathing. *Pobrecito.* Poor thing. None of this was Salvador's fault. He hadn't wanted to get into the car with Boss.

Delfino gritted his teeth. He was supposed to be the one with the brains, but he was always rushing into things and getting himself and Salvador both in trouble. Ever since they were little, Salvador's favorite saying, *Be patient*, had made Delfino hurry that much more.

Teresa had been patient, though. Delfino smiled, thinking of her gentle ways. She was only two years older than he was, but she had acted like she was much older. She looked out for him. She used to run off to see wildflowers or to point out a bird in flight and leave her meager food behind.

"Eat mine. I'm not hungry," she would call back. Now Delfino realized she had been depriving herself, to take care of him.

In Ahuelican, the lives of brothers and sisters were mostly separate after childhood, especially after marriage, and Teresa had married at fifteen. When Delfino came back from Mexico City and visited her, he wanted to cry at the sight of her thin shoulders and skinny legs and her stomach, just rounding. That was when he made up his mind to sneak across the border and earn some money fast. But he had rushed into a mess. Now he had to figure a way out.

Delfino slipped softly from his bed. All the men seemed to be sleeping heavily.

It was not a dark night. The moon and a sky full of stars shone through the three windows and the open door.

Delfino crept to the door. It was light enough for him to explore the grounds. He could find out a few things while no one was around to bother him. He could look the place over in private.

He pushed the screen open, squinching his face as it creaked. He stepped out softly.

Three shadowy forms lunged toward him growling—a growl that sounded like death. Yellow eyes glittered, and beneath them white fangs were bared.

His heart stopped. He gasped.

They were dogs, but dogs that looked like none he had ever seen. Delfino jumped back and closed the screen. They leaped at it, snarling. Their great teeth gleamed, and their neck ruffs stood up like lions' manes.

Delfino had never seen dogs like these. He didn't know what kind they were, but he knew that they could kill him. Their powerful jaws would stab sharp teeth into his flesh . . . would crush the bones underneath.

These dogs were not man's friend. They were full of hate and rage. They didn't bark, excited and pleased with themselves, like ordinary dogs. Instead, they growled, low menacing growls. These were dogs from hell. Guardians of the inferno.

A few of the men turned and muttered in their sleep. It was a sleep of exhaustion, or they would surely have been roused.

Could they just be indifferent? Or could it be that they were used to the sound of the dogs? Could such growls ever become familiar . . . ordinary?

Delfino slipped back to his cot. There was no way he could explore at night. He lay still, his heart pounding. Toward morning he slept.

He awoke with his hands over his ears. In his sleep he had been trying to shut out the clanging that seemed to burst in his brain—the sound of a bell, harsh, furious, jarring. A bell that belonged in hell with the dogs.

Salvador was touching Delfino's shoulder, his big hand gentle. "Come, Cousin," he said in his mild voice. "They are calling us awake."

Delfino got up. He patted Salvador on the arm, and they walked out to the water hydrant. They stood in line to wash. The sky that had shone so brightly in the star-filled night now looked pale and sickly. The men's movements were sickly, too, their motions stiff, heavy, sorrowful.

Delfino ate his rice and beans quickly. His stomach, tight and nervous, almost refused the food, but he knew he would need his strength. He forced down most of his plateful and was the first to finish. He walked into the yard to look around.

Slick was sitting on a bench outside the bunkhouse, smoking a cigarette. His gun rested on his knees. Delfino nodded to him, politely. He forced himself not to stare at the gun. He didn't want to show how much it frightened him, and he didn't want to make Slick mad. The incident with Lázaro had attracted too much attention already. Delfino wanted to fade into the background . . . to be noticed as little as possible.

"Buenos días. How are you, son? My name is José. They call me Uncle José." The speaker was an old man—too old for hard work.

"I'm Delfino." They shook hands. "I'm just trying to figure this place out."

"It is a place of great sadness."

Delfino felt Salvador's presence behind him. "This is my cousin, Salvador," he said without turning to look. "He can't talk to you. He only speaks Nahuatl."

Uncle José smiled at Salvador, and they clasped hands in silent greeting.

Delfino had been looking around the compound. He moved toward a pen where the dogs were fastened. Uncle José walked with him. Salvador followed several steps behind.

The dogs were pacing back and forth in the pen. Some were black and some were reddish brown. There was one big red dog, and one small white one. Hair grew in a thick mane around their necks. They had bluish-black tongues and were thickset and powerful. All but the little white one.

"Those dogs look like lions. What kind are they?"

"They call them chows. All I know is that they are *perros bravos*. Slick lets them out at night and fastens them up during the day."

"Grandfather taught me how to act with animals—how to be easy and how to sense what the animals are feeling, but I couldn't do it with these dogs. I tried to go out last night, and I thought they were going to kill me," Delfino said.

"Ay, son, believe your fear. These *perros* are ready to kill. Only a *momentito* with them and you'd be dead."

Although Delfino and Uncle José were at least twenty feet from the pen, and Salvador was even farther away, the dogs ruffled their fur and bared their teeth.

Delfino stopped walking. Disturbing the dogs would only draw Slick's attention to him again. Besides, even though they were penned up, the dogs made chills go down his spine. He couldn't help thinking what it would be like to have those sharp fangs tearing his throat.

Uncle José stopped beside Delfino, but Salvador brushed past them, walking quickly toward the pen.

Delfino started to shout a warning, but stifled his cry. Slick's attention could be more dangerous than the dogs.

Salvador stuck his arm in among the snarling dogs and began speaking softly in Nahuatl.

Delfino couldn't hear what Salvador was saying, but he knew that what the words meant wasn't important. The soothing sound was important. It was a bridge Salvador always used to reach animals—but these weren't ordinary animals. Delfino held his breath and stood frozen, watching.

Salvador kept speaking. His voice sounded like a caress.

The dogs stopped growling. Salvador touched one of them on the head. It made a plaintive, whimpering sound—a sound Delfino understood. What he had thought was a beast from hell was really a creature in misery.

"The dog is telling Salvador his grief," Delfino said. "Salvador learned Grandfather's lessons about animals better than I did. Animals trust him."

Uncle José nodded. "He is one of God's innocents. I saw it. His eyes are not in this world."

For a moment, Delfino wished he hadn't confided in Uncle José. He trusted too easily. Look what happened with the *coyote* and Boss. He told himself he should be on his guard, even among the other prisoners. But when he looked in Uncle José's lined face, he saw only kindness.

The other men had finished eating and were climbing on a truck. Slick shouted for Delfino, Uncle José, and Salvador to climb on, too. Delfino was glad to see that Slick's attention seemed to have been on the other men and on getting the truck loaded. He didn't think Slick had noticed Salvador talking to the dogs.

Their work was chopping weeds out of cotton. Each man was given a hoe and four rows to clean. Lázaro set the pace. He was clearly the strongest man in the group—powerful and quick. A kinder man would have set a pace that the others could follow easily, but the perverse Lázaro wanted to make things hard for them. The other workers were expected to keep up with him.

Slick followed the crew, mounted on a horse, his gun at hand.

It seemed to Delfino that they should all rush Slick at the same time. Thirteen men, hoes lifted . . .. But how many would be killed before Slick lay at their feet? And how many men might come to take Slick's place? If they succeeded in overpowering him, where would they go? How could so many men escape? Thirteen were too many—if you could even get them all to cooperate. Some seemed too downtrodden to rebel. Delfino would have to figure something out just for himself and Salvador.

Delfino paused and surveyed the land. It was flat, edged by a line of hills. There was no sign of a town or even a highway. Nothing lay between him and the ends of the earth, so where could he run? He couldn't even find his way back to the border. He had failed everyone—Teresa, Salvador, himself.

He felt like giving up. He wanted to lie down in a cotton row and cry. He had to force himself to lift his chin and his courage. He couldn't let himself give in any more than he could let himself act rashly. He had to be patient and watch for his chance.

Slick shouted something. Delfino couldn't hear what words he said, but he knew what the shout meant—*get busy.* He stepped forward and cut a weed. He must fit in, stay in the middle, be invisible.

A pickup with a water barrel and several dippers waited for them at the end of the row. Even Slick and Boss knew no man could work in this heat without plenty of water. Behind the wheel of the pickup was a man Delfino hadn't seen before. He stayed in the cab, smoking and looking straight ahead, not meeting the men's eyes, but Delfino could see that he was Hispanic.

The men crowded around the barrel. They elbowed each other out of the way, trying to be first.

Delfino and Salvador stood back and waited their turns, then went back to work. They were used to work. Delfino and Salvador knew how to ignore their bodies, how to put aching muscles and aching tiredness out of their minds—how to shut off their thoughts and keep working. Delfino knew that when you are in misery, if you must think, you do it on a different level—a level above tiredness, thirst, and pain—a level that looks from afar. That was how to get through weary hours.

Sweat dripped in Delfino's eyes. He wiped his forehead with his arm. The sun was no more than three hours high, but it beat with the intensity of midday. The sky above them seemed as flat as the fields. No floating clouds gave it depth.

"Slow down, Lázaro. You are killing us."

The brutish Lázaro grunted. Then he moved even faster.

"Hombre, we are men, not machines."

Delfino looked over at Uncle José. The old man staggered weakly. Delfino wondered if Uncle José would be able to keep the pace all day. Then he saw that Salvador was working the old man's rows as well as his own. That meant if Uncle José could endure walking in the heat, he'd make it through the day. What would happen if he collapsed? Or even if Slick noticed that he couldn't keep up? Delfino glanced toward Slick—Slick with the evil profile—Slick with the gun on his saddle. Delfino knew there would be no mercy.

The rows seemed endless. Heat waves danced before him and made him dizzy. He saw himself as if through an eagle's eye, alone in the vast cotton field, a small figure chopping weed after weed down an endless row. Strapped on his back were Salvador and Teresa.

Delfino shook his head, jarring himself out of his vision and back to reality. That vision was the path of his life, but it was a false and hateful vision of his sister and cousin as burdens. It was a self-pitying, hopeless vision. Delfino wouldn't let himself think like that—or be like that. And he wouldn't be a slave, either. He would find a way.

6

Enemies and Friends

By the end of the day, Delfino ached with tiredness, and pains shot up his neck like lightning flashes. He was glad to get back to the despised bunkhouse.

The sun was still two hours high when the truck brought them back to camp. They stopped outside the fence long enough for Slick to take up their hoes and carry them to one of two small wooden buildings. Delfino strained to see inside. It seemed to be a toolshed.

"What is that other little building?" Delfino asked Uncle José as they drove past.

"It is for the machine that makes electricity. Look." Uncle José gestured to wires coming from the building and running to the fence. "It is strong electricity."

Delfino didn't understand electricity. It scared him. Getting out of the fence was going to be hard.

This was the time of day, before supper and bed, when the men could wash and chat. They gathered around the hydrant or crouched in little bunches in the shade, but Uncle José, pale and barely lifting his feet off the ground, went into the bunkhouse without even pausing for a sip of water.

A couple of men joked at their own discomfort.

"Easy day, Carlos!"

"*Sí,* Oscar. A picnic!"

"For sure a picnic compared to breaking rocks," a sour-faced man named Silvestre responded. Someone else groaned.

Lázaro was walking around picking up small stones. Slick handed him a pack of cigarettes. Unlike the other men, Lázaro didn't seem tired, and he didn't seem to notice the sweat that had dried in dirty streaks on his face. He moved quickly, purposefully.

Delfino and Salvador sat on a couple of boulders that served for benches at the end of the bunkhouse. Salvador hadn't asked any questions. He seemed to accept what had happened as part of his fate.

"We need to watch the men," Delfino told him. "We have to observe what they are like, so we can figure out who to make friends with—who we can trust."

Salvador nodded, but Delfino realized that he might as well be speaking to the air. *Observe* and *figure out* were not the way Salvador decided things; he went by feelings. But right now Delfino didn't care whether Salvador paid attention or not. He wasn't talking to his cousin in order to really communicate but because it helped him keep his mind straight. By talking to Salvador, he could keep his thoughts reined in—keep them from racing round and round to a wild nowhere.

"Lázaro is at it again!" The bony-faced man Delfino had talked to the night before was speaking to a curly-haired youth. Delfino followed their gaze.

Lázaro was walking toward the dog pen. He put the rocks he had gathered on the ground near the fence. Then he picked one up and chunked it hard at a dog.

Delfino looked at Salvador, sitting beside him. His vague eyes were fixed on the distance. He appeared lost in his own world.

Lázaro threw again.

There was a sharp yelp. Then a snarl.

Delfino looked around. Where was Slick? He wouldn't leave until they were in the bunkhouse after supper. Surely he would stop Lázaro. Then Delfino saw him. He was watching Lázaro, a smile on his face.

Lázaro drew his arm back and threw hard. The little white dog wailed. Lázaro began to hurl rocks furiously. Dogs yelped in pain.

Suddenly aware of what was happening, Salvador leaped to his feet.

Delfino grabbed his cousin's arm, but Salvador jerked away and hurried toward the dog pen.

"Don't do anything, Salvador," Delfino said in Nahuatl. "We can't stop Lázaro. We can't think about the dogs. We have to think of ourselves."

Salvador didn't seem to hear him.

The dogs were barking and whining. Delfino knew he had to stop his cousin.

He ran after Salvador, gave a big jump, and leaped onto his back.

"Wait," he said in Salvador's ear. "Wait. We can't cause trouble. Not now."

Salvador ignored him. Carrying Delfino hardly seemed to slow him down.

Lázaro was throwing rock after rock at the dogs.

A horn sounded.

It was Boss in his white pickup with the red smudge on the fender. He got out, spat brown liquid, and swore. "What do you think you are doing?" he said to Lázaro in Spanish. "You're supposed to keep them dogs mean, not kill 'em."

Lázaro dropped the rock he held in his hand and remained standing, sullen and brutish, by the dog pen.

Delfino was still clinging to Salvador's back. "Stop," he said in Nahuatl. "Stop. Don't go to the dog pen. The dogs are okay. I don't want Boss to see . . ." He slipped to the ground as he spoke. "Careful," he added. "Careful. Let's go into the bunkhouse."

Boss gestured toward Delfino and Salvador. "Lázaro, you're not working the men hard enough, or they wouldn't feel like roughhousing. Step on it tomorrow. Push hard."

"You're supposed to keep him in line," Boss said to Slick, still speaking in Spanish. "You can't find dogs like these on every corner. If I lose one, I'll nail both your hides to the barn."

Slick's nod was a cringe. Lázaro stood unmoving and stolid. Boss turned to him. "There'll be a little sweetener for you this week."

Lázaro's dull countenance brightened.

"You hear, Slick? Shipment's coming."

"Yes, sir," Slick answered. His thin body curved into a servile position.

Boss turned. "Keep that ape in line. Now get the gate."

Slick ran to open it. Boss drove the pickup out.

Slick spit as he turned back into the compound. Salvador was at the dog pen, speaking comfortingly to the dogs. Delfino saw Slick look at him with an expression of hatred and malice.

Delfino joined Salvador. "Come on," he told his cousin. "Let's go check on Uncle José."

Salvador turned and followed him.

Delfino wondered how he could persuade Salvador to stay away from the dogs. The way he could communicate with them drew attention. It caused suspicion. Besides, Delfino began to wonder if Salvador's way with the dogs might be their ticket out of this place. He hadn't figured out just how they could use it yet, but he was sure he didn't want everyone to know about it.

Uncle José lay on his bed staring at the ceiling. "How are you, Uncle?" Delfino asked.

"Never mind," he answered. He lifted his hand slightly. "I was thinking about my daughter. She is beautiful as an angel, and as good." He smiled weakly. "I was wise enough to give her the perfect name—Angelina. She didn't want me to come to the States, but I didn't want to burden her. I thought I could work another season . . ."

Uncle José's voice faded, and he shook his head sadly. He closed his eyes for a moment. When he opened them, he said, "You must thank your cousin for helping me today." He turned his gaze to Salvador and nodded his thanks himself.

Salvador stood near the head of the bed—his youth beside José's age, his strong body beside José's frail one, his vague eyes beside José's alert ones. There was a bond between the old man and the young one, and there was some kind of communication even though they didn't speak the same language.

Delfino felt the need to say something. He searched his mind, but the only thing he could think of to talk about was what had just happened. So he told José about Lázaro, Slick, the dogs, and Boss.

The old man sighed. "Your cousin is going to suffer," he told Delfino. "Evil always despises good, and in this place, evil is in power."

Delfino didn't want to dwell on that thought. "It's time to eat," he said. "Let's go while there is still some food." He reached out his hand to help Uncle José up.

Uncle José made a small gesture, as though brushing away something of no importance. "Go on, son," he said. "Go on."

Delfino hesitated, then moved toward the door. "Supper time, Salvador," he said in Nahuatl. "We are late."

Most of the men were already eating. As Delfino stepped inside the building, the darkness of the big room with its single window and single light bulb seemed so eerie that the thought he didn't want to dwell on repeated itself like an echo: *In this place evil is in power.*

This looks like the Aztec underworld Grandfather used to tell me about, Delfino thought. The people here could almost be skeletons who have passed through the wind of knives and are ready to banquet with the Lord of the Dead.[1]

The men ate silently, their heads bowed over their plates while vague shadows rose and fell. It was hard to distinguish one man from another. Delfino had hoped to sit by the same man as the night before—the man with the bony, skull-like face whose name he had not asked. As he peered around the room, he felt an air of hostility. Were the men mad at him?

Delfino moved gingerly around the room. What was wrong?

It seemed like hours, though it could have only been a few moments, before he saw the man with the bony face and sat down beside him. Salvador sat across the table.

"Good evening, *compadre,"* Delfino said courteously.

The man gave a sharp nod and kept on eating.

"Is something wrong, *amigo?"* Delfino asked. "I feel that people are angry."

In the dim light, the man's eyes were deep as caverns. There was more weariness than anger in his voice. "What do you expect? You and your simpleminded cousin make things hard on us. Didn't you hear Boss tell Slick we have to go faster, all because you imbeciles were acting like clowns?"

For a moment, Delfino felt as if his blood had stopped coursing through his veins. Had everyone in camp turned against them already? Boss, Slick, and Lázaro were all the enemies he and Salvador needed. Life was hard enough without having the other men against them.

"Friend, surely, the fault was Lázaro's. Why do you blame us and not him?"

"Because we know Lázaro for the devil he is," the man answered, "but we didn't know you two would add to our pain."

The man picked up his plate and moved away. Delfino stared after him, an empty feeling in his stomach that had nothing to do with food.

He turned to look at Salvador and saw that he, too, was leaving. He was walking out of the building carrying a plate of food.

"What do you think you are you doing?" a voice shouted in Spanish. It was Slick calling to Salvador. "You can't take food out of here."

Slick was standing in the wide door where he could see both inside where the men were eating and outside into the compound. He walked toward Salvador as he spoke. Salvador brushed past him, his vague eyes looking toward the bunkhouse.

Delfino jumped up and hurried to the door. Salvador was already halfway across the lot.

"He doesn't understand," Delfino told Slick. "My cousin doesn't speak Spanish. And he's a little . . . strange. I'll explain that he has to eat in here. I'll bring the plate back."

Slick glared at Delfino and did not answer.

"Please excuse me," Delfino went on. "I'll go after him." He trotted toward the bunkhouse, hating himself with each step. It was humiliating to humble himself to a lowlife like Slick, but he didn't have a choice. Even after stooping as he had, he knew that Slick would make them pay. He also knew that it would be easy for Slick to shoot both him and Salvador out in the field when they were working. He could just tell Boss they were trying to run away.

When Delfino entered the bunkhouse, he saw Salvador, his hands under Uncle José's arms, helping him into a sitting position. Then Salvador crouched on one knee and began to feed Uncle José. The old man chewed slowly. The muscles in his thin neck tightened as he swallowed.

Delfino stood still. It was not a moment to interrupt. Color began to return to the old man's face. When he gestured that he was finished, Salvador put the plate aside. Then he unfastened Uncle José's sandals and helped him lie back down.

Now Delfino could take the plate back. He had been afraid that Slick would follow him into the bunkhouse to get it, and he wondered why he hadn't. Maybe something else took his attention, or maybe he just didn't want to bother. Delfino was thankful that Uncle José's meal had not been interrupted, but he knew that now Slick had one more thing against them.

It wasn't long until all the men went into the bunkhouse for the night. The dogs were let out, and Slick left. Most of the men went directly to bed.

Delfino decided to lie awake and make plans. His eyes felt dry and gritty—like there was sand in them. He closed them for a moment.

He awoke with a start and realized he must have been sleeping for hours. It was a starry, moonlit night. He looked toward Salvador's cot. It was empty. Had something terrible happened to his cousin while Delfino was sleeping? Maybe not. Maybe he was with Uncle José.

Delfino got up and walked through the bunkhouse very quietly. Uncle José was sleeping, and Salvador was nowhere to be seen. Delfino crept to the door, remembering the dogs' fury the night before. But he had to find Salvador.

He opened the screen very slowly.

No dog barked.

He put one nervous foot out.

No dog growled or lunged.

Delfino stepped outside. The heavens were ablaze with stars.

How is it that the world is so beautiful and so horrible all at once? he thought.

He wanted to lose himself in the fresh night air and in the starry sky above, but he forced his eyes to earth and began his search. At the end of the bunkhouse, he saw the dogs, huddled together, sleeping. He went closer, fearful with each step.

Then he saw Salvador. The dogs were curled around him, and Salvador was asleep amidst the dogs.

7

A Dog Named Bandit, a Friend Named Valente

"What are you doing out here?" Delfino whispered.

"Just sleeping." Salvador sat up.

Delfino saw that he had taken his blanket outside with him.

"Don't you know you'll get in trouble?"

"The dogs were sad. They need me."

The dogs were awake. They lay quietly, calmly, like resting lions, but their alert ears were up. They seemed nothing like the dogs from hell they had been last night. Only one of them looked at Delfino suspiciously, his neck hair raised, but even one was enough to make Delfino nervous.

The big red one began rolling onto his back, making happy sounds. Delfino had noticed before that although this dog was big, he was young—not a pup, but young enough to be playful. He began frolicking. He caught one corner of Salvador's blanket, jerked it free, and ran across the compound.

Salvador smiled. His usually impassive face lighted up. He jumped to his feet and ran after the dog. The other dogs followed at his heels. Delfino was left standing alone as Salvador and the dogs romped.

What in God's name am I going to do, Delfino thought. How can I take care of this big child?

Salvador recovered the blanket and returned. The dogs were so close around him that he bumped them with every step.

"We'll call the red one Tlashtehqui," Salvador said quietly, "because he stole the blanket."

Delfino nodded and smiled. It was a good name because Tlashtehqui meant bandit in Nahuatl.

"I call the little white one Ychcaconetl," Salvador said.

Delfino smiled. Ychcaconetl meant Lamb. Even though he was worried about their very survival, Delfino couldn't be angry at his cousin for finding a bit of joy.

"Let's sit down over here," he said. "I want to talk to you." He picked a spot that would be out of the view of anyone at the bunkhouse door.

"Salvador, I don't want everyone to know about your way with the dogs. It is better for us if they don't know. Can you stay away from the dogs in the day and only come out here when everyone is asleep? Can you come back inside before daylight?"

Salvador nodded.

Delfino knew that such a plan wouldn't stay secret long, but he also knew he wouldn't be able to keep Salvador away from the dogs entirely. He had to compromise.

Delfino touched his cousin on the shoulder and repeated his directions. Then he went back to the bunkhouse.

He felt a little better. Being able to sneak out at night was a big step toward freedom. The next step was to figure out how to get out of the electric fence. But he knew he had to be careful. There was no room to make a mistake.

He opened the door to the bunkhouse very quietly. It squeaked. He closed it softly and stood stock still in the doorway, barely breathing. Although the moonlight shone through the windows, it was darker inside than it was out under the stars, and Delfino waited a few moments for his eyes to get used to the change. He looked at the men resting in their beds. Some of them moved a little, but most of them remained motionless. Then Delfino saw a pair of eyes fixed on him.

"Just getting a breath of air," Delfino whispered.

There was no reply. Suddenly, he realized that the owner of those eyes was in the same bunk he himself had lain in when he first arrived. The eyes belonged to Lázaro.

Delfino froze in place. Could Lázaro have been spying on him through the bunkhouse door?

He slipped softly into bed, but he couldn't rest. He felt that an evil animal, more powerful than the dogs, lay in wait, watching for the right moment to pounce on him.

The next day's work was again chopping weeds out of cotton in what seemed endless fields. Lázaro set a brisk pace, faster than the day before, and Delfino could feel the hostility of the men toward him and Salvador. He could only hope they would soon get over their anger.

Delfino and Salvador managed to get positions on either side of Uncle José so they could both help work his rows. The heat was dreadful. To Delfino, the sun was like a fierce eye glaring down on them, scorching them with hate. The day was their enemy, the night their friend. It would be during a friendly night that they would break away from this place, but Delfino had to find out more about the fence. And he needed to know which way a town was.

The men crowded around the water barrel at the end of the rows just as they had the day before. Again Delfino stepped back and waited. He was trying not to irritate any of them. He knew he needed a friend. Salvador and Uncle José stood back, too. The first group of men drank. Some of them splashed their faces. Some poured water over their heads.

Slick rode forward on his horse. The men stepped aside. Slick rode up to the barrel and let his horse drink.

The men who were about to drink waited, their eyes on the ground. They were slaves, but they were not dead to insult.

Only the horse was drinking. Salvador went forward, took a dipper, and reached it deep in the barrel, speaking to the horse gently in Nahuatl as he did so. "I must take water, brother, and give it to my ancient friend."

The horse paused and looked directly at Salvador. Slick's face hardened.

Salvador gave the dipper of water to Uncle José. Slick narrowed his eyes, but Salvador took no notice.

Slick hates Salvador for being good and because Salvador doesn't take him into account, Delfino thought. Salvador doesn't care about Slick, and he knows it. Salvador didn't mind the horse, either. Slick hates him for that, too.

"The evil one is thinking of a way to hurt your cousin," Uncle José said softly to Delfino. "He will think of something—something we couldn't expect."

Delfino nodded. That was one more reason to hurry up and break out of here.

He took his turn and drank, but he didn't speak until they were far down the cotton rows and out of Slick's hearing. "What do you know about the fence, Uncle?"

"I only know that the ground is too packed and hard to dig underneath it in one night—at least without tools. And I know it is electric. One man died climbing it."

That was the same thing the bony-faced man had told him. Delfino tried to think of another way he could get out. Maybe he could hide under Boss's pickup without his knowing it. That would be hard. Delfino cut a big weed with an angry chop.

When they had hoed another round and were again at the water barrel, Delfino saw that Slick was not there. The Hispanic driver was alone. This time he was out of the pickup, and he had Slick's gun. He was beefy and his shirt, wet with sweat, clung to his thick back.

Delfino had hoped that he would find some fellow feeling in the man. He had hoped that he could count on his sympathy later on. He had even imagined that it was shame or sorrow that had kept the driver looking straight ahead without meeting the workers' eyes the day before. Now he knew that wasn't the reason. The reason he hadn't met their eyes was simply that he didn't care. The driver's expression was stupid and without compassion. But maybe that meant the man would be easier to trick than Slick. Maybe he was the weak link in the chain that bound them.

Delfino felt like running, but he could almost hear Grandfather's voice advising him to be cautious. "Our forefathers, the old men, the old women, the white-haired ones said that while we travel on earth, we live along a mountain peak. Over here there is an abyss; over there is another abyss. If you go astray from the middle path, you will fall and plunge into the deep."[1]

"Why don't any of the men run now?" Delfino asked Uncle José.

"They don't know where to go," Uncle José answered. "They don't know this country."

Like me. They don't know any more than I do, Delfino thought.

Later, outside the bunkhouse, he was waiting his turn to wash when Slick drove up in yet another pickup. A young man got out quite casually and walked in the gate after Slick, his eyes ranging around the area.

He hasn't been here before, Delfino thought, and he doesn't know what kind of place this is.

The sun shone on the youth's face. It was intelligent, relaxed, assured.

Slick fastened the gate.

The young man sauntered across the yard in his crisp new pants, and glanced at the watch on his arm. Delfino approached him and spoke. *"Buenas tardes.* I am Delfino." The young man stretched out his hand. "I am Valente. I am from Monterrey."

His handshake was firm and friendly.

"Are you legal?"

"No, no. Illegal. I slipped across to visit my brother in Abilene. My brother has a green card, but he found a place where I can work without one. I did it last summer, too."

"Tough luck that you wound up here."

"Why? The man who gave me a ride said he had to make this detour. It won't take long, and then we'll be gone. He is going all the way to San Antonio."

"He lied to you. He's the devil's right-hand man. You are in a slave camp. They snatch up illegals and bring them here to work."

"No lo creo. I don't believe it." Valente glanced around, located Slick, went over to him, and began to speak in Spanish. Delfino watched, feeling anxious for the likeable Valente.

"How much longer are we going to be here? If you are going to be a while, I'll just head on by myself. I'm itchy to hit the road."

Slick looked down at Valente, and smiled an evil, gloating smile—a smile that would infuriate anyone. "Don't seem to me that's a good idea. My idea is that you stay the night." Slick called over his shoulder, "Lázaro!"

Delfino's heart skipped a beat.

Lázaro was at Slick's side in a moment. He pinned Valente's arms behind him while Slick reached into his pockets. He took Valente's billfold and change.

Valente struggled. "What are you doing? Give me my money! Give me back my photos!"

"Okay, Lázaro, let him go."

As soon as he was released, Valente swung at Slick.

Slick easily avoided the blow.

Lázaro doubled his fists, an expression of pleasure on his face, but before he could strike, Delfino was beside Valente. He put his arm around Valente's shoulders and led him away.

"Why did you do that?" Valente asked angrily. He turned to Salvador. "You're a big guy. Why didn't you help me fight?"

"He doesn't understand you," Delfino explained. "My cousin, Salvador, only speaks Nahuatl."

"He is so strong—why didn't he help me fight them? Why didn't you?"

"Because we couldn't win. They have guns. They have everything. We can't waste ourselves on fights we'd lose."

Uncle José moved near them. "Delfino is right, son," he said.

"I'd rather die fighting than give up."

"We haven't given up, but you can't fight these guys head on. They'd as soon kill you as look at you. Maybe rather. We have to wait. We have to make a plan."

"They took my money. They even took my photos. They didn't leave me anything."

Just then Boss drove up. He parked outside the compound beside Slick's pickup.

Slick hurried to open the gate. Boss stepped in. His eyes were on Valente. He was angry. He pushed his hat back on his head and began talking to Slick in rapid English.

"I'd give anything if I could understand them," Delfino told Valente.

Valente turned so Boss and Slick couldn't see his face and began to translate. He spoke very softly, at almost the same time as Boss and Slick. Delfino could see the gestures that went with the words. He felt almost like he was hearing Boss and Slick.

"What do you mean bringing someone like that out here?" Boss's fat face was red.

Slick, thin and cringing, answered, "Boss, he is just another wetback. A young, healthy one."

"Look at him, you fool. He's not a simple peon from the South. He's probably got family along the border who'll look for him."

"Well, Boss, he asked me for a ride. You said you'd need more men and some smart ones to build the airstrip. It seemed like . . ."

Boss swore a string of oaths.

"You want me to take him back?"

Boss half turned away in exasperation.

"I'm working with idiots! You can't take him back. He knows this place now, and there's no telling what those last two troublemakers have told him."

Salvador turned toward the bunkhouse. "I'm going to rest," he said in Nahuatl.

Delfino knew Salvador didn't understand anything that was being said. He nodded, still listening to Valente translate.

"Did you get his money and I.D.?"

"Yes, sir. Boss, I could take him out in the night. He wouldn't know the way."

"He wouldn't have to, you imbecile. If he told the law, they'd find us. Now that you've got him, we'll have to keep him, and you'll have to watch him like a hawk."

Boss showed his disgust by spitting a long stream of brown liquid. "And don't blow your top again. If this one has to be killed, I'll kill him myself."

The color drained from Valente's face. His voice shook as he translated.

Boss turned away from Slick and gestured toward the gate. Slick opened it, and Boss walked out swearing. He got in his pickup, slammed the door, and roared away, leaving a cloud of dust behind.

Slick's expression changed to one of malice.

Delfino knew from his face that something terrible was going to happen.

"Lázaro!" Slick called. "Lázaro!"

8

Salvador Risks All

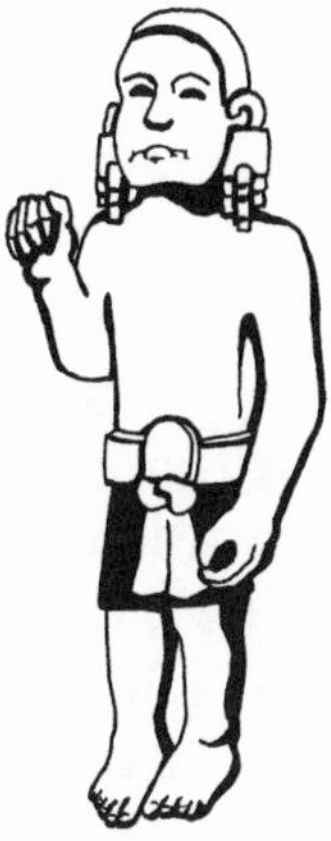

"Slick is going to do something evil," Uncle José said.

"Get some more rocks," Slick said to Lázaro. He went to his pickup and got out a box and a gun. It wasn't the rifle he used to guard the men.

"Por Dios!" Delfino exclaimed. "Is he going to kill . . . ?"

Uncle José interrupted. "Not kill," he said. "That is a shotgun, and that box is full of shells he has filled with rock salt."

Delfino couldn't make sense out of what Uncle José was saying. Salt didn't sound bad, but he knew it had to be.

Lázaro went behind the bunkhouse where rocks and broken concrete were piled. He began to bring buckets full of rocks and put them with a pile he had gathered before. "Hit the same one I hit," Slick said to Lázaro.

He aimed and shot Bandit.

Bandit howled.

Lázaro threw a rock. It hit Bandit hard on the hip.

Delfino had a sick feeling in his stomach.

Slick aimed at Bandit again, and Lázaro followed with another rock. He hit Bandit on the head. The dog ran back and forth in confusion.

Slick began shouting, *"El negro!" "El moreno!" "La blanca!"* "The black!" "The brown!" "The white! Let's give the white one a fit!" Lázaro hurled rocks in rapid fire as Slick shot.

"I don't understand," Delfino said. "Slick shoots them, but they don't bleed."

"It's because he's using rock salt," Uncle José said, shaking his head sadly. "It gets in the skin and hurts like fire."

The small white dog Salvador called Lamb ran in a circle yelping, as gunshots and rocks hit her over and over.

Then Slick and Lázaro began hitting the dogs randomly. The dogs ran, leaped, whined, snarled in a frenzy—all but Lamb, who now lay in a corner whimpering. Every few minutes, they hit her again.

Slick's face was fixed in a grin.

Delfino was revolted. He didn't feel he was looking at a man. He felt he was watching a being that was less than human, and he was in that being's power.

"It doesn't matter if we kill that white one," Slick said to Lázaro as he threw another rock. "It's too little to be worth anything." The dog lay on her belly, drooling and whining.

Delfino pitied the poor animal. He hoped Salvador had fallen into a sound sleep. There was no telling what he would do if he saw what was happening.

But Salvador wasn't asleep. He came out the bunkhouse door. He stood on the step looking across the compound where men were gathered in groups, all staring toward the dog pen. It took Salvador a few moments to realize that the dogs were being tormented.

He ran toward the pen.

Delfino followed, his heart racing.

He knew he couldn't stop Salvador this time. He also knew there wouldn't be much chance of helping against whatever meanness Slick turned on Salvador, but he could try. And he could stand with him. Salvador had always stood with him.

Now Slick was shooting at the dogs from one direction, and Lázaro was throwing from another. The animals snarled and bit each other.

Salvador reached the pen. He stretched his hand toward the latch. It had a padlock on it.

He started climbing the gate.

One part of Delfino felt that he should go with Salvador. Another part thought that would be foolish. And he was afraid.

He heard the men in the compound muttering to each other.

"The dogs will tear him up."

"Doesn't he know he'll be killed?"

Delfino felt as if his blood were draining out of his body, leaving him a weak shell.

Lázaro threw a rock and struck Salvador on the shoulder. Slick shot him broad in the back. Salvador didn't react. He swung his leg over the top of the gate.

Delfino knew he should be with Salvador, but his feet were like iron welded to the place where he stood. He heard the men's comments.

"Maybe he's too dumb to be scared."

"Too dumb to know what hurts."

Lázaro threw a couple of hard ones. He hit Salvador on the shoulder and on the head. Salvador kept to his course. He leaped in among the pain-maddened dogs and spoke to them in Nahuatl—spoke in his gentle crooning voice. The dogs grew calm. They pressed around his legs, whimpering mournfully.

Salvador went to the corner where Lamb lay. He picked her up and cradled her in his arms. Slick blasted his back again. A rock hit him on the cheek. He turned and faced Slick and Lázaro. On his face was the acceptance of death.

He is like a captured Aztec warrior, Delfino thought. He embraces destiny.[1]

Slick lowered his gun. He must have seen how little anything that he could do to Salvador mattered to him. *"Basta,"* he said to Lázaro, who was reaching for another rock. Enough.

"Salvador is God's child," Uncle José said.

The men in the compound had fallen silent. One said, "We have seen a miracle." He crossed himself.

So much for our secret about Salvador's way with the dogs, Delfino thought. "They'll probably put a man with a gun in the compound at night now," he said aloud.

"I doubt it," Uncle José responded. "Slick won't want Boss to know what he did. He's in trouble already."

Delfino walked to the pen. Salvador had sat down with Lamb close beside him, her head on his knee. The other dogs huddled close.

"Are you okay?" Delfino asked in Nahuatl.

Salvador nodded. Delfino thought he saw pity in Salvador's eyes. He pities me because I was afraid to stand with him and embrace destiny.

He flushed and turned away, ashamed and angry. He was ashamed to have been a coward, ashamed not to have faced Slick inside the pen with his cousin, and angry that he felt ashamed. Why should he risk pain or even death with nothing to gain? It didn't make any sense. Not any sense at all.

"Let's leave him in peace," he said to Valente and Uncle José. "He wants to be alone with the animals."

Delfino's anger faded as quickly as it had flushed his cheeks. Salvador is braver than I'll ever be, he admitted to himself, and he has a purer heart. Grandfather would be proud of him.

"I don't understand your cousin," Valente told Delfino later as he sat on his cot. "Why would he risk his life just for an animal? I have to tell you, I think that's dumb."

"It's not dumb! Salvador respects animals. That's what Grandfather taught us." Delfino spoke heatedly. He didn't like to hear his cousin criticized. Then Delfino softened his tone. "Grandfather said we should give reverence to every single creature. For us, the dog is the most important of all."

"It is? My family doesn't even like dogs."

"Well, we do. Dogs are our companions. It was always like that with the Aztecs. Grandfather said that a dog accompanies us into the underworld when we die. He goes as our guide and to be our companion there. That's why . . ." Delfino's voice trailed off. He hesitated to finish his sentence. Was he revealing too much?

"Why what?" Valente seemed sincerely interested. His gaze was frank and open.

"That's why our people used to be buried with a dog. It was with a red dog, in fact."[2]

"A *red* dog?"

"Yeah. I don't know why."

"I didn't mean to insult your cousin. I shouldn't have said *dumb*."

Delfino remembered that he had used that word, too—in his thoughts. He was sorry he had ever felt that way about Salvador, even for a minute, even in secret.

"I have to admit he is strange," Delfino answered. "He is hard for people to understand—even hard for me sometimes. It's true that he doesn't have a quick head, but he has a wise heart, and even if he can't speak Spanish, he sure can talk to animals."

The bell sounded for supper. Delfino went to the dog pen. Lamb's coat was wet, and Salvador was washing his own rock salt wounds at the water spigot. His cheek was bruised and swollen.

"Come, Salvador. Let's eat."

Salvador rinsed his hands and face. Then he climbed over the fence.

They were the last ones in line. The eating barn fell into silence when they entered.

They sat with Uncle José and Valente and ate in silence. Delfino had many things he wanted to say to Valente, but he couldn't do it now when everybody would hear. He could feel Slick's eyes boring into his back. Slick would think of something dreadful to do to them. Something unexpected and deadly.

Delfino felt a hand on his shoulder. He looked up. It was the bony-faced man. "I was wrong to be angry before. I'm sorry," he said. "My name is Eduardo. They call me Lalo." He held out his hand, first to Salvador, then to Delfino. He went back to his place, and they finished eating in silence. But the silence seemed friendlier—except for Lázaro's sullen glances and Slick's hate-filled stare.

Delfino could hardly wait to talk to Valente in private. He hoped that they could slip into the yard while the others were sleeping. He felt sure that with Valente's help, he could work out an escape plan. He could see that Valente was smart—he even spoke English—and he had been on this side of the river before. Together they would find a way.

That night, Delfino stayed awake easily. He lay perfectly still, listening, intent. All his senses converted into hearing.

The men coughed and turned restlessly. It seemed like hours before the only sounds in the room were the soft rhythmic ones of steady breathing. Delfino got up slowly, moving with painstaking caution. He touched Valente's arm and barely whispered, "Come."

They moved so lightly no board creaked, but Delfino thought he saw Lázaro's eyes open. His blood turned to ice. He grabbed Valente's shoulder, and they stood stock still, not even breathing. Lázaro didn't stir.

Delfino and Valente went out the door. A dog growled, but Salvador, who was again bedded down with the pack, sat up and spoke softly in Nahuatl, and the dog was silent. Delfino and Valente walked toward him. The dogs bristled, but Salvador spoke soothingly to them again.

"I need to talk to Valente," Delfino told Salvador. "I don't want anyone to know. Don't let anyone come out."

Salvador nodded and moved slightly so as to more easily see the door. One arm rested on Lamb. The low moon behind him formed a halo. The moonlight glowed on Lamb's white hair and reflected upward to Salvador's face. He was bathed in silver radiance.

Delfino was aware of the gulf between that peaceful scene and their reality. They were trapped in hell.

"Being taken as slaves doesn't seem possible, not even after what I saw this afternoon," Valente said. "Not even after what I heard. That scared me plenty, and I'm still scared. But it doesn't seem like real life. It's more like a movie."

"It's real all right. I've been trying to figure out how to get away. I don't know how to get out, and I wouldn't know which way to go if I did."

Valente looked around, taking his bearings. He pointed to the east. "There's a railroad that way."

"There is?"

"Yes. I'm sure it's that way. We could hop a freight train. Lots of wets hop that train."

Delfino breathed deeply. He felt as if a heavy boulder had rolled off his shoulders.

"Let's scale the fence and take off. It will be easy," Valente said.

"Not so easy," Delfino answered. "It's wired with electricity. Strong electricity. One man died on it."

"Then we'll have to short it out."

Delfino gasped. "You know how?"

"Maybe . . . not exactly, but I think I can figure something out."

Delfino looked through the fence and across the fields to the mountains beyond. The moonlight lent them a mystic glow.

Out there lies the Promised Land, he thought. Maybe I'll get there yet. Maybe I can still help Teresa.

The heavens seemed filled with stars, but darkness lay over the northern sky. Thunder rumbled in the distance, and lightning flashed.

9

Eavesdropping and Spying

The next morning, Boss was at the compound before they even had breakfast. As they went to eat, Delfino knew that Valente was straining to hear what Boss was telling Slick, but his face was perfectly blank.

Valente is a good actor, Delfino thought. He doesn't let it show that he can understand.

Delfino could hardly eat, but he forced himself. He knew he had to keep up his strength; he was skinny enough already. He wanted to ask Valente what was happening, but he had to wait for the right moment. If he didn't, one of the other workers might overhear, and even they must not know that Valente could speak English. Such downtrodden men might betray them for the comfort of no more than a pack of cigarettes.

At last the moment came. "What was Boss saying?" Delfino asked under his breath.

"He said that a plane is coming in tonight and that he needs a load of rocks. That doesn't make good sense to me. I don't see what the rocks have to do with the airplane."

Neither did Delfino, but he was about to decide that nothing made good sense. Why would a person have slaves when people like himself and Salvador were willing to work for peanuts? Uncle José had said evil was in power here. Delfino believed he was right and that Boss and Slick did evil things just because they had evil hearts.

When they left the eating barn, Delfino noticed a different pickup truck outside the compound–a nice clean blue one. A tall American stood beside it, looking up at the fence. Delfino knew that man! He was Buck. They had seen him at the restaurant when they first met Boss. Now Boss went outside to talk to him.

The low embers of hope in Delfino's heart leaped into a flame. Maybe Buck would help them.

Delfino put his mouth to Valente's ear. "Go listen to them! Pretend you are looking for something."

Delfino looked the other way, and Valente went near the two Americans. Later he told Delfino, "I didn't hear very much. Nothing that seemed important. The man asked Boss about the electric wires, and Boss said that some of his big dogs would climb the fence if he didn't have them. He asked about the rocks piled over by the dog pen, and Boss said he was going to mix concrete. Then I left because Boss was looking at me. They drove off before I got to the bunkhouse."

Was that all? Oh, if only Delfino knew English, maybe he could have heard more. Maybe he would have shouted to Buck, "Help! Help us!" But why hadn't he shouted in Spanish? He could have. Now the moment was gone. The hope that had flamed in Delfino's heart sank as if smothered by a boulder. Buck was gone and they were on their own. But they made a plan. That night they would watch for the airplane. They would take shifts.

It was a hard day. Lázaro worked them double time. Poor Uncle José could hardly totter fast enough to keep up, even though the three boys worked his rows and even though Lalo helped some. Delfino could feel Slick's eyes on him, and Lázaro's glance was full of hatred. How long could they live like this?

Something was surely going to happen. That night, for the first time since the boys arrived, the dogs weren't let out of their pens, so Salvador slept in the bunkhouse, too.

They were all exhausted by the brutal work pace. Delfino could hardly stay awake for his turn to watch. Then sleep came on him, heavy and hard, burying him under a weight of unconsciousness. When Valente shook his shoulder, he could barely lift that smothering weight.

"It's here! I saw the plane land!"

Delfino struggled out of bed and hurried to the window as fast as his stone feet would move.

"It's behind the building where we eat."

All Delfino could see was that the lights were on. The door where they always entered to eat was closed, but light shone around it, and light shone out of the lone window.

"Let's sneak over and look in," Delfino told Valente. "But let me wake Salvador first. He can keep the dogs quiet."

The three boys slipped out of the bunkhouse. Salvador ran softly ahead and climbed into the dog pen. Delfino and Valente moved slowly toward the window. Delfino knew he must not go too fast.

Slow down. Be careful. Be careful, he kept telling himself.

When they peeped in the window, they saw that the big door on the opposite side was open. Lázaro and someone Delfino hadn't seen before were carrying in some crates.

Boss and Slick were there, too. Boss pried a box open and took out a package; it was about the size of a brick and was wrapped in dark plastic.

Boss sat at a table, his back to the window. Slick sat across from him. Boss was so big, he blocked the view. Delfino couldn't tell what they were doing, but he saw Boss hand Lázaro a small packet. Lázaro snatched it eagerly.

Valente pulled at Delfino's sleeve. "Come on," he said. "Let's get away from here!"

"What were they doing, Valente?" Delfino whispered. The three boys were standing close together outside the bunkhouse. "Or do you know?"

"I know," Valente answered. "I wish I didn't, and I'm not going to tell you. You're better off not knowing. It's the devil's work."

How could it be better not to know? Delfino didn't understand. He didn't argue, though. He just sank into his bunk, his heart drumming a funeral march.

10

Devil Mountains and Devil Work

"Six men is enough, George," Slick said to the beefy Mexican-American driver the next morning. "Take these." And he tapped Delfino on the shoulder. He also tapped Valente, Salvador, and three others—Carlos, Oscar, and Silvestre—the same three men who had talked about rocks earlier. "We need the rest of the men to get this stuff ready."

"We're going to the devil today!" Carlos said with a bitter grin as they climbed in the bed of the pickup. "That's the *Sierra del Diablo.*" He gestured toward a line of mountains with low foothills.

"You mean it's the *Sierra del Diablo Boss*, the Mountains of the Boss Devil," Delfino answered, making his own small joke.

The hills stretched some miles—blue lumps on a yellow-brown plain. Delfino wondered if they might have to hide there when they broke away from the camp. Could they follow the hills and get to the railroad?

When the pickup stopped, Carlos said, "Here we are at the Devil's Half Acre." That remark seemed more truth than joke. Two great holes gaped at them like stone jaws—the stone jaws of the Devil and of death itself.

Piles of bone-colored rocks lay in a row. George backed the pickup to one of the piles and handed each of them a shovel. "Load 'em!" he said.

For the millionth time in his life, Delfino wished he were bigger and stronger. His light, skinny body wasn't good for this work. He tried to make up for his size by working smart and using leverage, but in an hour he was staggering.

Slick arrived in another pickup that was already half full of something, but Delfino couldn't see what it was because there was a tarp stretched across it. Slick ordered the men to load rocks on top of the tarp. They heaped the bed high until it was completely loaded and the tarp could not be seen.

"I'm heading to San Antone with this load now," Slick told George. "Boss will take his truck to Houston. He's meeting Pino."

Delfino listened. What Slick said didn't mean a lot to him, but he saw Valente turn pale. Delfino also saw that Salvador looked sad. "What's wrong, Cousin?" he asked.

"I'm afraid for Uncle José. How can he do his work without me?"

Delfino wanted to say something comforting in response. "Lalo will help him. Besides, from what Slick said, I don't think they are working in the field today. We'll probably be back with him tomorrow," he told Salvador.

Slick drove off in the loaded pickup. George told the men they could rest until another pickup came to be loaded. Delfino had a chance to look around a little bit. A big, tall machine stood near a deep hole. The machine seemed to be made for lifting heavy squares of rock. The walls of the hole were straight and clean—machine-cut. A second hole was only about ten feet deep. It was clean-cut, too, but there were small uneven rocks in it, like the ones they were loading.

Tired as he was, Delfino wanted to look around more. They needed to know as much about the area as they could. George dozed on the seat of the pickup he brought them in; the men sat on the ground.

"Let's take a walk!" Delfino said.

"You're a crazy man. I don't want to go wandering through scrub brush," Carlos said. "It's nap time for me." He stretched out on the ground. Silvestre and Oscar didn't want to go either.

They shook their heads at Delfino, but Valente and Salvador followed him. Valente looked worried.

"What's wrong?" Delfino asked.

"I've heard of this man Pino," Valente said. "His name is Agripino Elizondo. He's bad news. Real bad. We've got to get out of here fast."

"Well, now is our chance to look for a place to hide when we make our break," Delfino replied.

It was hard to walk in the scrub brush, and they were all ready to jump out of their skins. Even so, Delfino couldn't help noticing the beautiful view. The earth was red-gold; the hills were blue; white clouds rested on the mountains beyond. He took a deep breath. There across the plain lay his future.

George's angry voice called, "Hey! Where'd you go? Get back here!"

Delfino turned back. Brush crunched underfoot and dragged at his legs as he hurried. He pushed a waist-high bush aside. Then something shifted under his foot.

The earth dropped away, and Delfino found himself falling deep into darkness, surely, he thought, to his death, to the cold land of skull-faced Mictlantecuhtli with its owls and spiders. . . . [1]

Delfino hit the ground. He lay there for a moment, struggling to get his breath. Above him, maybe two men high, was a round patch of light. He wasn't dead. He had found not Mictlantecuhtli's underworld, but a cave. This might be the hiding place they needed.

Valente was calling, "Hey, where are you, Delfino?"

Delfino shouted in answer, but his voice sounded muffled.

The opening to the cave was only about a yard across, and went straight down. There wasn't much light, and Delfino couldn't tell how wide or long it was. He knew he shouldn't go exploring there alone. If he fell down another hole, he might not make it out. Still, he couldn't resist trying to discover a little more.

Delfino heard Salvador calling in Nahuatl, "Cousin, where are you? The man is calling us back."

"I'm down here," Delfino answered.

He couldn't leave. Not yet. Slowly, his eyes got used to the dimness. He felt the earth carefully with each foot before putting his weight down. Maybe someone had hidden gold or silver in the cave. Maybe he would find it. His *tonali* would change. He'd have money for Teresa.

He saw a dark shape against the wall. What was it? A chest on end?

Delfino squatted close to it. He strained to make out the shape in front of him, then stifled a scream.

Before him sat a skeleton with its legs casually crossed. It had on cowboy boots and Western clothes. A round badge was pinned to the shirt.

He went closer to get a better look. The cowboy hat was pushed back and great empty eye sockets stared at Delfino.

Then he saw the hole in the forehead.

Had this man had been murdered? Shot in the head?

Delfino turned and ran. He scrambled up the wall, digging his hands into the earth.

"Salvador! Valente! Wait for me."

George was yelling for them to come. When they got to him, his face was sweaty and red with anger. "Where were you?" he shouted. Delfino thought he saw fear as well as anger on George's heavy face. Then, for no reason, George raised his hand and struck Salvador a heavy blow.

Salvador looked at George mildly. His vague eyes seemed to see into and through him.

George took a step back.

Delfino felt a new weight of guilt fall on his back like bone-colored rock. It was his fault they were late, and now he couldn't help his cousin. He wanted to hit George with a shovel. He wanted to bash in his thick head.

Why had George picked on Salvador? Delfino thought Salvador's goodness made wicked people mad. But Salvador's like Quetzalcoatl, Delfino thought. No matter how the evil magicians tormented Quetzalcoatl, he wouldn't hurt anyone.[2]

Delfino could see Valente clenching his fists and gritting his teeth. Even Carlos and the other men wore angry expressions. Delfino thought if he raised a shovel the others might follow him. For sure, everyone except Salvador would like to see George's blood flow.

But they might not follow Delfino's lead, and even if they did, Delfino doubted that they could survive hiding in the hills. They would die for lack of water, or Slick would find them. To fight now was the sure way to die later. So Delfino just touched his cousin's shoulder gently and went back to work. He boiled with guilty rage, and he was shaken from seeing the skeleton.

It was comforting to be beside Salvador and Valente. Even sweating as a slave wasn't so bad with your friend and cousin beside you—not as bad as being alone in the dark with a murdered skeleton.

When they finally quit for the day, they had loaded two more trucks, one of them Boss's big white pickup with the red smudge on the fender. Even after such a hard day, good-natured Carlos still had the strength to joke. "Don't fall in a hole! The devil will get you and throw your bones in his bone pile!"

Carlos didn't know how true his joke was. Delfino grinned weakly at the irony, but he couldn't think of a response. He was beyond joking. What he felt was more than exhaustion, more than the humiliation of being enslaved, or even the crushing weight of guilt. It was more even than the horror of the murdered skeleton. To him, the loaded trucks seemed like big dung beetles crawling across the prairie with their disgusting load. He felt that he was a part of something dirty—something he didn't comprehend but which made him feel unclean.

11

The Bones of the Dead

The next morning they were taken back to the field. Hoeing cotton wasn't hard compared to loading rock.

"Don't ask any questions about yesterday," Valente warned Delfino quietly. "You don't want to know any more than you have to." As they rode to the field, he began to ask Uncle José about the weather.

"It's the season of storms," Uncle José said. He gestured toward thunderheads in the distance.

Delfino wanted to talk to Valente about how they could escape. He wished Valente knew Nahuatl. If he did, no one but Salvador would understand them when they talked.

"Last year there were big winds. And lightning. And hail," Uncle José said.

Delfino turned to Valente and started to speak. But Valente held up his hand as a signal to be quiet. Delfino couldn't understand why Valente was talking about the weather.

"Uncle, was it this time of year when the storms came?"

"Yes," Uncle José said. "It was dry a long time, like it is now. Then there were storms."

"And there was a lot of lightning?" Valente seemed very interested.

"The most lightning I have seen in all my years. The farm, these fields . . . the lightning loves the earth around here. I saw a man get struck last year. It is a horrible way to die."

"How about the electricity? Did it go out?"

Now Delfino understood what Valente was getting at. He didn't know much about electricity, but he knew it went off during storms. That used to happen all the time in his *barrio* in Mexico City.

"Yes, son. We were without lights for more than a day."

Delfino's eyes met Valente's. They didn't need to say a word. They both understood what they had to do. They had to wait for nature to help them. When there was a storm and the electricity went off, they could scale the fence. Delfino would watch the sky more intensely than he ever had in his life.

Delfino's spirits lifted. A storm was sure to come. They just had to be ready for it. When the truck stopped, Delfino leaped out almost as lightly as if he were working for wages.

He glanced back and saw Salvador standing at the tailgate reaching up to help Uncle José.

Lázaro was watching Salvador, too. Delfino felt uneasy.

As Salvador's hand touched Uncle José's, Lázaro kneed Salvador hard in the back.

Salvador staggered and fell. His hand jerked out of Uncle José's, and Uncle José hit the ground hard. His face twisted with pain.

Delfino felt the jab as if he had been struck himself. He ran to his cousin.

Slick watched from his horse, smiling. George, who had driven them to the field, took no notice.

This is how they will punish Salvador for his goodness, Delfino realized. They'll do it through Uncle José.

Salvador got to his feet, and he and Delfino helped Uncle José to his. The old man grimaced and moaned softly as he took a step.

Salvador, his arm around Uncle José, fixed his distant eyes on Lázaro. His mild gaze seemed to see into Lázaro's heart. Salvador spoke softly in Nahuatl. "You are lost. Small and lost."

Lázaro couldn't understand the words, but Delfino felt that he took the meaning. At least he knew that, do his worst, he could not pull Salvador down.

Lázaro growled a curse.

Slick rode closer. "That's enough. Anyone fighting gets shot. You hear that, you Injun troublemaker? Okay, get moving!"

Salvador didn't react. Delfino was sure that being ignored again would make Slick even madder. There was no telling what he would do next or what Lázaro would do.

The men hurried to the field, but Salvador walked slowly, helping Uncle José.

Slick nodded to Lázaro and patted his gun.

Delfino felt sick. How could he possibly protect Salvador?

No breeze stirred. The still air lay on them like a blanket. They could hardly breathe. Above them the sky was dotted with fluffy, innocent clouds. But to the north it was dark, banked with dense, black clouds that rose like mountains. An occasional flash of lightning zigzagged through them.

"Tlaloc and his children are smashing water jars in the north," Salvador said.[1]

"Yes," Delfino answered. "Pray for rain."

As soon as the words were out of his mouth he wished he had said *hope* instead of *pray,* but in truth, his hope was as intense as a prayer, Aztec or Christian.

"Tlaloc sends terrible rains from the north," Salvador said, as if reminding Delfino. "Those rains hold the bones of the dead."

Delfino nodded. He knew. He wanted a storm.

He and Salvador had placed themselves on either side of the old man as usual, but today that didn't last long. When they finished the first lap, Lázaro pushed in front of Delfino. He was going to try to start a fight, Delfino was sure.

Uncle José moaned. It wrenched Delfino's heart to see him drag his injured leg up and down the rows. He thought about Grandfather and how terrible it would have been for him to be in a place like this. He was grateful that Grandfather had died at home and that he'd had grandsons to care for him and respect him. Uncle José was old and alone.

They hadn't worked long before Lázaro thrust his hoe in front of the old man. Uncle José stumbled. Lázaro chopped the ground around the old man's feet, sometimes hitting in front of them, sometimes behind or between them. "Dance, old man," Lázaro laughed. "Why don't you dance?"

The men, working scattered across the field, noticed and shook their heads. Lalo swore, his bony face angry.

Lázaro shoved his hoe between the old man's legs and tripped him.

Salvador reached Uncle José as he fell and caught him. Then he put himself between the old man and Lázaro. Uncle José used his hoe like a cane and kept his hand on Salvador's arm.

Delfino knew Salvador would protect Uncle José at any cost. This was a scheme to justify killing Salvador.

Lázaro circled behind them. He chopped at the old man's legs and ankles, wounding them. Uncle José cried out. Salvador leapt toward Lázaro.

The innocent blue sky grew suddenly dark. A strong, cold wind, thick with dust, swept in.

Slick yelled and waved for everyone to come back to the pickup. The men tried to hurry, taking awkward, spraddle-legged steps in order to stay on their feet. They seemed to blow toward the truck rather than move by their own power.

Salvador picked Uncle José up and carried him in a staggering run. The old man's legs and feet were bleeding.

The rain hit as the men scrambled into the pickup.

Hail began to fall. "The bones of the dead," Salvador repeated.

12

Free at Last

The men huddled together, shoulders hunched and heads down. Back at the compound, they slogged to the bunkhouse, already too wet to bother hurrying any more.

The boys helped Uncle José to his bunk. Salvador found an old bucket and filled it. Then he knelt in front of Uncle José and washed the blood and dirt from the old man's wounded feet and legs.

Delfino looked at the men around him and thought, These are men without hope, in a place without hope. That's what Padre Ignacio used to say hell is. A place without hope.

Delfino sighed at his own musings. Here I am thinking like a Christian. Christian, Aztec, the border between them is confusing, but I can't bother about that now.

He sat on his cot, his back against the wall, waiting for the moment. He wished he and Valente had had a chance to plan, but they couldn't talk now. They could only watch.

The men sat still and despondent, or moved about the room aimlessly on stiff feet. Delfino wished he could help them, but he had all his skinny shoulders could carry.

He had to think of Salvador, of Teresa, of himself.

Uncle José moaned. The old man lay on his side, his eyes closed, his face pained.

Valente stood staring out the window. The rain fell in solid sheets, and there was nothing to see, but Delfino knew he was watching for the lightning that would set them free.

When everyone went to bed, Delfino lay down, too, but he lay awake. He heard Salvador get up and move toward the door. Delfino sighed. He knew Salvador was going out to be with the dogs. He got up and followed his cousin outside. Rain was still falling, but the makeshift porch provided the dogs with some shelter. Lightning flashed.

A loud clap of thunder followed. The dogs whined, growled, and snapped at each other. In the eerie light, Salvador moved toward them.

"Salvador, you can't stay out here in this weather," Delfino said.

"The dogs are afraid of the lightning and thunder." There seemed to be a rainbow over Salvador's head. It made Delfino think of Quetzalcoatl's beautiful feather headdress.

The dogs surrounded Salvador, bumping against his legs and making complaining noises. All but Lamb. She looked up at Salvador from where she lay against the bunkhouse. Salvador crouched beside her and scratched behind her ears. "Ychcaconetl is sick," he said.

Delfino had seen earlier from Lamb's eyes that she was not just hurt, but was also ill.

Suddenly, the dogs bristled and growled. Delfino eased closer to Salvador for protection.

Salvador spoke, but this time the dogs ignored him. What if he lost control of them? They were dreadful creatures at best. Now, excited by the storm, they might even turn on Salvador himself.

Suddenly, Bandit leaped toward the door. The other dogs followed, their fangs bared. Delfino's pulse pounded in his temples. These were the dogs from hell he had seen the first night—fearful, monstrous bone-crushers.

Barking and growling furiously, the dogs sounded like they were about to tear someone's heart out—someone who was at the door.

Lightning flashed.

It was Lázaro in the doorway.

It's not just the storm, Delfino thought. The dogs hate their tormentor. But Delfino was afraid for himself. He imagined his soft throat ripped out by cruel fangs, and his spindly grasshopper legs crushed between fierce teeth.

Lázaro moved back.

Salvador spoke a command, and the dogs returned to him.

Delfino wanted to get in out of the rain, but he was afraid Lázaro would pounce on him. If Lázaro hurt him, he wouldn't be able to escape. So he waited. At last, he walked toward the door, stepping cautiously. Any stray gesture or sudden movement could rouse the dogs and be his doom.

He made it safely to his bunk. Valente was still at the window. The sky was wild with lightning, and thunder rocked through the heavens. A loud sound—a different sound, like an explosion —jarred the building. Delfino flinched. Lightning had struck very close. Something had been hit.

All the men sat up in their cots, exclaiming.

"Now, Delfino! Now!" Valente whispered. He grabbed Delfino's arm and pulled him toward the door. "I saw it strike. Lightning hit the generator. We can climb the fence."

Someone tried to turn on the light and complained that there was no electricity. The men crowded to the windows.

Delfino and Valente slipped outside.

"Come on, Salvador! This is our chance. We can climb the fence now. We've got to run."

"What about the dogs?"

"We can't take the dogs. Come on!"

"I can't leave Lamb. And what about Uncle José?"

"Cousin, we're trying to save our lives. Come on!"

"Uncle José and Lamb need me."

"We can't make it with a hurt old man and a sick dog." Delfino couldn't stand still. His feet moved in place, and his body twitched.

"Salvador, your kind heart will kill you. And kill me too!" Delfino knew what he said was true. Sometimes you need to be hard and practical. You even need to be mean, or at least cold. If you want to survive, it has to be like that. He wasn't like the old Aztecs. He didn't want to be a dead warrior, noble or not. He longed to live.

"Salvador, it's time to save yourself!"

A weak voice spoke. "Salvador, you must go." It was Uncle José. He had followed them out. "Delfino, tell him I speak with the authority of my years. He must go. I command it."

Frantic as he was, Delfino felt a slow warm flush of gratitude that Uncle José had understood the situation. He translated the old man's words into Nahuatl.

Valente had already climbed the fence and leaped down on the other side. He ran to the shed and came back carrying tools.

"I'll cut a hole with these wire cutters, so the old man can come through," he said. He worked quickly, like a person who knew what he was doing.

"Come on through this hole," Delfino told Salvador. But Salvador pushed Uncle José toward the opening.

The old man's injured leg faltered, and he stumbled. "No," Uncle José said. "You'd never make it with me. Go."

Delfino translated, but Salvador still did not move. Delfino was pushing his cousin, but it was like pushing a stone wall.

"Tell him by going he might save us all," Uncle José said. "If he is free, he can tell the authorities. He can get help."

Delfino translated again, but without much hope. If Salvador didn't come now, Delfino would leave him behind—he'd have to.

But Salvador nodded when Delfino translated Uncle José's last speech. Delfino felt a flood of relief.

The dogs were leaping and snarling, maddened by the thunder.

Salvador spoke to them, and they grew calm.

Increíble! Delfino thought. For frenzied wild dogs to become instantly calm wasn't normal. All Grandfather's teaching had not prepared him for this. It was like a miracle. Delfino half expected Salvador to raise his hand and calm the storm as well.

Valente thrust a screwdriver in Delfino's hand. "Here's your weapon. Come on! Run!"

Delfino ran. "Follow me!" he called over his shoulder to Salvador.

Valente was already well ahead, running like the wind, a pickax on his shoulder. Delfino hadn't gone far when he realized that Salvador wasn't with him.

He stopped and looked back. He saw shadows move at the fence. A great flash of lightning zigzagged across the sky. Salvador was inside the fence struggling with Lázaro!

Delfino ran toward his cousin. A yell rose from deep inside him. A mighty clap of thunder rocked the heavens. It seemed to be his own enraged and anguished cry. He raced through the rain, the screwdriver in front of him ready to sink it into Lázaro's heart.

Lázaro's hands were at Salvador's throat. Salvador wrenched free. Lázaro slipped and fell to the ground. Bandit leaped on top of him.

Salvador jumped through the hole in the fence, then looked back. He must have spoken to Bandit. The dog froze.

What would Bandit do? He seemed pulled by opposite emotions—hate and love. Did Bandit want to kill his tormentor more than he wanted to follow his master? He was only a beast, and his blood was up.

At last, as though breaking a chain that bound him, Bandit sprang through the hole. Together he and Salvador ran toward Delfino.

Lightning flashed, illuminating earth and sky.

A scream cut through the air before the rumble of thunder followed.

The other dogs were on Lázaro! All of them! Delfino's visions of sharp teeth sinking into a soft throat, of torn flesh, of crushed bones, were really happening, to Lázaro.

Salvador saw, too, and started to turn back.

He would try to help the devil himself, Delfino thought. "It's too late," he shouted. "He's lost already, and we need to get help for Uncle José."

Salvador and Bandit ran back toward him. Delfino waited for his cousin. They would run together. That was safer. Salvador was too kind for his own good, but even Delfino felt a surge of pity. To be torn apart by dogs was a terrible death, even for a brute.

There was no time to think about that. No time to even worry about being followed. Not yet. The only thing to think about now was running—running hard into the cutting rain—running between lightning bolts—running for freedom—running for life.

Three boys and a dog ran like antelope, racing toward their destinies, or toward their fate.

13

Paradise Found

Delfino felt that Tlaloc was hurling thunderbolts at him. At last the lightning and thunder ceased, and there was only a driving rain. It beat against his face. It hammered against his chest. It pushed against his steps.

At last, toward morning, it stopped. His clothes hung heavy and dripping, but simply to be free of the pelting drops made him feel unburdened. His steps soared.

The boys ran till dawn. Valente led, and they raced across fields, down a dirt road, and finally onto a hard surface. Morning came with a gradual increase of light and revealed a sodden world and a pale sky that had spent all its power.

The three boys stopped without a word and looked around. Bandit drank from a puddle. Valente leaned on the pickax handle.

"You carried a heavy weapon," Delfino said, indicating the pick.

"We're going to need it," Valente answered. His eyes were searching the distance.

"What are you looking for?" Delfino asked.

"I don't know exactly," Valente answered. "I have to find something familiar. Then I can figure out where we are."

He didn't sound worried, but Delfino felt a moment of doubt. Maybe Valente didn't know this area well enough after all. Maybe Slick or Boss would find them before they could get to the railroad.

There were no crops in view. Only grassland dotted with mesquite and an occasional grazing cow.

"This will lead us to a railroad track," Valente said. "It's bound to. All we have to do is follow it."

"Follow it and watch for the Border Patrol. And for Slick and Boss," Delfino added. "We are so tired from running in the rain, we'd be easy to catch."

Delfino had said *catch* but he thought *kill.* He didn't much mind being caught by the Border Patrol. If it weren't for Teresa he wouldn't care at all. But Boss was something else.

The land was so flat they could be seen for miles, and Boss could come riding up at any moment, but they had decided the hills weren't really an option. Valente didn't think he could find a railroad in that direction, and he was afraid they would get lost. Delfino didn't argue; after seeing the skeleton in the cave, he hadn't been keen to go back to the hills. He clasped the handle of the screwdriver that was in his pocket.

Not a bad weapon, he thought, and the pickax is even better. They're not much against a gun, though.

Delfino wondered what was happening back at the farm. How was Uncle José? Perhaps other men had braved the dogs and had escaped through the fence. Or perhaps seeing what happened to Lázaro frightened them too much, and they were all still in the compound. Or maybe the dogs had gone through the hole and were ranging the countryside. By now Boss would have come to the farm and found Lázaro's body—what remained of it. Delfino shuddered as he thought about Lázaro.

"Lázaro chose his own death," Delfino told Valente.

"Yeah. He got what he deserved," Valente answered.

Delfino couldn't help thinking about the dead man in the cave. He couldn't say that man had deserved his death. Maybe he didn't. Delfino looked at Salvador and Valente. Boss would kill them all if he could, and they didn't deserve to die. That man with the badge on his chest had been murdered. No one had buried him with respect. Maybe there was no one to feed his ghost on the Day of the Dead.[1] Maybe he was in dim, cold

Mictlan, his empty skull-eyes staring at Mictlantecuhtli's skull-face. That was too horrible. Delfino didn't want to think about that man and his terrible *tonali;* he wanted things to be fair.

"The Aztecs would say a dreadful death was Lázaro's fate, his *tonali,*" Delfino said to Valente. "My Grandfather always talked about fate, but I never believed in it."

"Why not?"

Delfino thought about that. "I guess I never wanted to believe in it," he admitted. "I want to control my own destiny."

Delfino remembered how he had once been so caught up in tussling with the idea of *tonali* that he had failed to show proper respect and had argued with Grandfather, but Grandfather had not taken offense. He knew Delfino didn't mean to be rude—knew that he was only trying to understand.

"How can there be fate if you make your own destiny?" he had demanded.

"Be patient," Grandfather had said, using the phrase that became Salvador's favorite. "Some day you will see how these things fit together."

Now trudging down a foreign road, thinking about the death of Lázaro, Delfino felt that he was beginning to see into the mystery. Lázaro had made his own destiny by being what he was, but his death was his fate. Could that be what Grandfather meant?

"Have you gone to dreamland?" Valente joked. He pointed to a sign on the road ahead: Mexican Hat 15 miles. "That's where we'll hop a freight train."

"Good news, Salvador," Delfino said in Nahuatl. "We're almost out of the wilderness. There's a town ahead."

Salvador nodded in response. The nod seemed to be in slow motion. Fatigue weighed on them all.

Valente staggered. The pickax he carried seemed to tip his balance. Salvador took it from him and carried it.

"We've got to rest," Delfino said. "Fifteen more miles and we won't be able to stand up, much less climb in a freight car."

"If we had something to eat we could keep going," Valente said.

Delfino wished Valente hadn't mentioned food. He had been trying to push the thought of it out of his mind.

My stomach has grown to my backbone, he thought.

It might be that Bandit could catch a rabbit, although the dog was as tired as they were and walked with his head drooping. They could lie in wait, throw something, and kill a rabbit themselves, but that would take time, and they had to hurry. Besides, even if they could risk the attention the smoke would attract, they didn't have any way to make a fire. They didn't have any matches, and all the twigs and pieces of wood were wet. They had nothing but the pickax to use as a knife.

I'm not starved enough for raw rabbit yet, Delfino thought. His empty stomach turned. Nausea and weakness overcame him, and he had to stop walking for a few moments.

They were thirsty, too. Delfino had decided that he would drink from the ditch at the side of the road as soon as they came to a place where the standing water looked at all clear. They had walked out of the area of the heaviest rain, and the only water was some muddy puddles.

A white farmhouse lay ahead. It was solid and substantial, with a wide porch and a well-kept lawn.

"You speak English," Delfino told Valente. "You could ask for water. Maybe they'd let us work for some food."

Valente laughed. "If I look anything like you do, they'd think I was a bandido and shoot me."

Delfino grinned. Valente saw the funny side of things, and he was right about how they looked. Delfino couldn't imagine how they would ever make themselves presentable enough for human company. Even handsome Valente, who had had a watch and stylish pants, really did look like a bandido now. And Salvador, with his hair grown long and tangled, mud on his clothes, and his vacant gaze, was a sight that would scare the bravest man—especially with Bandit beside him.

So instead of stopping for help, they picked up their pace as they passed the house. It was set well back from the road, but they were careful not to look in that direction as they went by. They did not want to give any indication that they even thought of going near it. They didn't want to cause alarm. But no one seemed to notice them. On the few occasions when a car passed, they kept their eyes straight ahead.

Salvador was still carrying the pickax. About half a mile down the road, he pointed with his free hand, indicating a field. The field was cultivated, not rangeland like they had been seeing for so long. What was growing there?

As they drew closer, Delfino could see that it was a watermelon patch. Suddenly he was running. It was not an act of will. His stomach was in control. It was a puppeteer pulling the strings to his skinny legs. He ran to the field and bent over the nearest melon. He was about to pick it up and drop it to break it open, but before he could do that, he felt Salvador's hand on his shoulder.

"Be patient, Cousin. Wait a moment."

Salvador found a melon that had released the vine. He thumped it, and it sounded hollow so he cut it with the pick, making a precise line down the middle, cutting through the rind and into the meat. Then he pulled it apart and revealed its secret interior.

It was red and dripping with life. Salvador broke the melon into four parts, and the boys dug into the sweet meat with their hands. The melon was still cool from the night. Bandit, as hungry as they, ate just as greedily.

It seemed to Delfino that the sweet pieces he broke off and put into his mouth were absorbed even before he swallowed. He felt his strength returning with each bite.

They ate two melons. Then they were satisfied.

They dug a hole and buried the rinds. The soil where the watermelons grew was sandy and not entirely sodden. Still, the boys got muddy, and they were sticky from the melon.

"We've got to find some water," Delfino said in Spanish. "We can't go into town like this. We've got to wash."

"I know," Valente answered. "I keep thinking we will find a place where the livestock get water."

They started back down the road. Delfino had thought that if he had something to eat, he would be strong enough to keep going. He did feel stronger, but now that his hunger was satisfied, another need, just as profound, took its place—the need for sleep. Every few minutes he had to give his head a shake to keep himself awake.

I guess I'm a real sleepwalker, he joked to himself, unable even to say the words out loud.

He stumbled and almost fell. The third time he stumbled, he knew he could not go on. It was dangerous to sleep. You were vulnerable then, but Delfino had to take the chance.

"I've got to rest." He said it both in Spanish and in Nahuatl. "I don't think I can keep going."

"Me neither," Valente said. "The shape we're in, we couldn't protect ourselves from a mosquito. Three zombies and a zombie dog, that's us."

"Let's go over there." Delfino spoke in both languages again. He indicated a clump of mesquite bushes on a rise.

Without waiting for an answer, he started toward it. When they reached the mesquite, they looked down on a pond. The high ground where the mesquite grew must have come from the pond when it was dug. Delfino could hardly believe their good luck.

The pond was large and irregular in shape, its edges graceful as rippling water, or as the leaves of the water plants that created little green islands topped by white flowers. White cattle with humps on their backs drank at the pond's edge. Most wonderful of all, it felt safe because it couldn't be seen from the road.

"Did you ever wonder what paradise looks like?" Valente quipped as he jounced down the slope, taking quick, stub-toed steps. He pulled his shirt off as he went.

"This pond looks like the sacred *cenote*[2] Grandfather told us about," Salvador said.

Delfino nodded. Grandfather had talked about the deep pool dedicated to Quetzalcoatl. People threw their gifts to the gentle god into that *cenote.*

They washed their clothes and themselves. The pond was deep enough for Bandit to take a swim. He shook himself and sat on his haunches panting happily—laughing his doggy laugh.

Bandit hasn't had much to be happy about before, Delfino thought. Now with Salvador, things will be better for him.

They lay down in the shade of the mesquites and slept the sleep of angels, deep and untroubled.

When they awoke, it was late afternoon—the bright late afternoon that goes with long summer days. They lingered, enjoying the tranquility, but Delfino's enjoyment was bittersweet. He couldn't forget the men and dogs still trapped in the camp, especially Uncle José and Lamb. He knew Salvador was worried, too.

Salvador and Bandit had gone back down the slope to the water's edge. Salvador took some of the sticky, half-dried mud, shaped it into a figure, and threw it into the pond. Delfino knew he was making an offering. Then Salvador and Bandit sat together, boy and dog, watching the minnows swim and watching the dragonflies hover over the water.

"If it were just me and Salvador, I'd have to take a chance, go up to a house, and ask for work even though I can't speak English," Delfino said. "Not that they'd be likely to hire us, the way we look, so it's a good thing you have a better plan. Tell me what you have in mind."

"When we get to Mexican Hat, we'll hide in a boxcar."

"Yes, but where will the train take us?"

"It doesn't matter. Anywhere is good as long as it is north or east, but the train will probably go to San Antonio or maybe Houston. We can lose ourselves in one of the big *barrios* there."

"What about your brother?"

"He's a lot farther north. He's in Abilene. If I call him, he'll come get us, but first I want to get some miles between us and Boss."

He said *us*, Delfino thought. He didn't say 'He'll come get *me*.' He said *us*.

Delfino took a deep breath. Once more, Valente made him feel as if a burden had been taken from him.

"I don't think my skinny legs will get so tired anymore," he said, "because they won't have so much to carry. You just took a big load off my back."

Valente laughed.

He was a true friend, and Delfino was lucky to have him. He wanted to tell Valente, wanted to express his appreciation.

"In my village, they say a person's *tonali* stays with him forever. I have a good *tonali,* a lucky one. Having you for a pal proves it."

"Por Dios! Is there no justice? Am I destined to be hooked up with you forever?"

They both laughed. The laughter spread through Delfino's body in a healing flood.

Salvador and Bandit had climbed back up the ledge. Salvador surveyed the landscape, looking away from the pond and toward the highway. He dropped to his knees and hunkered down behind some mesquite brush.

"It's him," Salvador said in Nahuatl. "It's Boss."

Delfino didn't bother to translate. He lay flat, only stretching his neck up to peer down at the highway. Against the sun he could see a white pickup exactly like Boss's. In it was a big man, his Stetson set at a familiar angle.

It was Boss.

14

Wings and Greens

They waited for dark, but it fell slowly. Their glimpse of Boss had broken the mellow tranquility of the place. Images flashed in Delfino's mind—images of what would happen if Boss caught them. He wouldn't just take them back as slaves. He would think they were too dangerous. Besides, Boss was mean and vengeful. He would certainly kill them just like he had said he would. Maybe he'd put a gun to their heads, one by one, and they'd end up like the skeleton in the cave.

Delfino's thoughts made him shudder, but the landscape looked as peaceful as before. Nothing moved except the soft-eyed cows that walked around slowly, gently chewing their cud, and the occasional birds that dived down to the water to drink or splash.

At last, almost in unison, the boys gestured that it was time to move on. They ate another watermelon, this time leaving the rind for the cows. No one mentioned Boss again.

The heavens burst into a red sunset, the color coming suddenly and covering the whole of the western sky.

"The women are using bright blankets to cover the sun," Salvador said. His face wore a tender expression, as it often did when he mentioned something he had learned from Grandfather.

Salvador's expression caught Valente's eye. "What did he say?" he asked Delfino.

Delfino translated what Salvador said. Then he explained.

"The old Aztecs said that warriors who died in battle rise with the sun and go with him through the sky to the peak of his journey. Eagles fly with them and are their messengers. At noon, the spirits of women who died in childbirth take the warriors' place and go down the sky with the sun. At sunset, they lay him to rest for the night in bright blankets."[1]

Mention of women dying in childbirth brought Delfino's worst fear to mind. Teresa might die in childbirth.

Valente put the pickax on his shoulder. "Tell your cousin I'm rested. It's only fair that I carry the ax now."

Delfino translated what Valente said, but he knew that the real reason Valente wanted to carry the pickax was different. The real reason was that he didn't trust Salvador to use it—not even against Boss or Slick. He thought Salvador was too gentle and dreamy, and that his head was too full of strange beliefs. Valente wouldn't hesitate to use the ax, though. Neither would Delfino. He grasped the screwdriver in his pocket and held it firmly for a moment as they made their way to the road. He hoped they wouldn't meet Boss, but if they did, he was ready.

"I sure wish that farmer had planted a little corn beside the watermelons," Delfino remarked. "My stomach needs something solid to work on."

"Don't even mention it," Valente answered, "unless you want to see a young man cry."

Delfino smiled. Valente was tough, but he always had a joke. The jokes reminded him of Carlos, who was so lighthearted and brave. It hurt Delfino to think of him still at the camp. But he had to push that out of his mind.

"At least we look a little more presentable since we washed," he said.

"I'll tell you the truth," Valente responded, "when we get to Mexican Hat, a pretty girl isn't going to ask any of us to dance."

Delfino laughed. "Maybe she won't scream when she sees us, at least." He scratched his head. His hair felt crusty. Bathing without soap didn't do much for hair, especially when you didn't have a comb.

They lapsed into silence. The road ahead seemed endless. It was a ribbon unwinding before them in the moonlight.

Is this road a good emblem for *tonali?* Delfino wondered. We didn't choose it. We took the only road there was. Perhaps Grandfather would say the road itself is our fate. But is where we follow it our destiny?

But Delfino didn't want to start thinking about destiny now. Danger lurked around every corner; he needed to keep his attention on what was going on right now.

The steady rhythm of their steps was hypnotic. Delfino heard nothing else, was scarcely aware of anything else for miles. He tried to stay alert, but he lost himself in his steps. One more step. One more. One more. Step. Step. Step.

Suddenly Delfino's stomach contracted. It grabbed so violently, it shocked him into alertness. He smelled food. Beans. Bandit ran toward the odor, but Salvador spoke to him, and he fell back.

They were on the outskirts of a settlement. It must be Mexican Hat.

"I think that's a restaurant ahead," Valente said, pointing. "I think that's a sign on that building, but I can't read what it says. If it's a cafe, we'll go around to the back when we get there. They will have thrown away some food, for sure."

Hunger had made Delfino's nose keen, and the odor carried to him on the breeze was so achingly strong, it seemed that the restaurant must be very near—but it wasn't.

The boys walked faster, lassoed by the aroma. They were close to it before they could read the small lighted sign: Wings and Greens.

"I think they sell *pollo y verduras,*" Valente said.

It was a very small restaurant. When they reached it, they went to the back, and Valente looked in the garbage bin. "They must have thrown away some bread, at least," he said.

Delfino tried to look over Valente's shoulder into the bin.

A deep voice spoke in English. "What you boys think you doin'?"

Delfino wanted to run, but the aroma of food tied him in place. He looked toward the voice and saw white clothes—long white pants and a white T-shirt stretched over bulging muscles. It took him a minute to see the face and hands. They were black.

Bandit growled—a fierce growl that rumbled in his throat. His neck hair stood up. He bared his teeth and stood ready to lunge. He was a dog from hell again.

"Call off your dog, now. How can I feed you if you scare me like that?"

Valente translated to Delfino and gestured to Salvador. Salvador spoke to Bandit.

"We just wanted what you were throwing away," Valente said. "We are so hungry."

The black man answered.

Delfino wished he could understand what was being said. He felt vulnerable and powerless.

The black man's teeth flashed in a smile. Valente laughed.

"What's he saying?"

"He said I can't bring the pickax in the restaurant. He's going to feed us inside. Tell Salvador he has to leave the dog out here."

The kitchen was small and tidy. A mop stood in a bucket of water. A pot of beans bubbled on the stove. Delfino walked through the restaurant looking to see that no one was hiding there. He checked that the front door was locked. The man watched him, an indulgent expression on his face.

The man gestured, indicating the restroom. Delfino went in first, glad for the chance to wash with soap. There was a mirror above the washbasin. The round face and dark oval eyes that looked back at him wore a hard, determined expression. The straight black hair that framed them was tangled and long.

A strange-looking comb lay by the washbasin. It had widely spaced teeth. Delfino filled the basin with water, thrust his head in, and worked up a lather.

"Hombre!" Valente called. "Don't be so slow!"

"Un momento," Delfino answered. He rinsed his hair and combed it with the wide-toothed comb, but he couldn't get all the tangles out.

When he came out, the black man handed him a plate of food. Mashed potatoes were piled high. There were some cooked greens along with a couple of chicken wings, and a spoonful of beans.

The man was talking in a lively way, and Valente put in an occasional word between bites, no longer interested in washing. Salvador went into the bathroom.

"What's he telling you?" Delfino asked Valente.

"Oh, nothing much. He stayed late to clean the kitchen and to cook beans for tomorrow. Mexican Hat is another fifteen miles. This is just a village."

Salvador came back and nodded his thanks when he took his plate. Then he started to the door.

The black man said something.

"He says Salvador should sit in here. He has some scraps for the dog, too."

When Delfino translated, Salvador nodded again. But he didn't sit down.

The black man saw that Salvador was waiting for the dog food. He laughed, took the lid off a metal can, and used a cup to dip food scraps into a bowl. He handed the bowl to Salvador.

Salvador took the bowl outside to Bandit, and sat on the step to eat his own meal.

"This man takes the restaurant scraps home to his pigs," Valente explained. "That's why he puts the food people leave on their plates in a can like that."

"We need to tell him about Boss and the slave camp," Delfino said.

Valente nodded. "Give me time."

Delfino sat on a stool at the counter with his feet on the stool's foot rail. His thin knees stuck up and out. He thought he must look like a grasshopper on top of a post.

Then as Valente ate, he and the man began to talk again. They sat across from each other at a small work table.

The food was wonderful—even the half-done beans—but Delfino felt awkward. He hated not knowing what was said. It made him feel left out and small.

Is that how Salvador feels all the time? Delfino wondered. He never knows what is being said since no one but me speaks Nahuatl. Delfino felt a pang of pity and understanding for Salvador's isolation. He felt a pang of guilt as well. He couldn't forget that he had let his cousin stand alone in the dog pen or that he had been ready to leave him behind.

Valente finished eating. He was talking animatedly in English.

"Oh, Lord! I thought those slaving days were over," the black man exclaimed. "Of course you can use my phone."

"He's going to let me call my brother in Abilene," Valente told Delfino.

The words *call my brother* were just what Delfino had been wanting to hear. Valente's brother with his real job and his green card seemed like a hero to him—a person with knowledge and power, a man in charge of his destiny. Since he had a place for Valente to work, he might know where there was work for Delfino and Salvador, too. Even the town where he lived sounded romantic—Abilene. He whispered it over and over to himself as Valente dialed. Abilene was north, far from Slick and Boss and the Border Patrol. It was the town of Delfino's dreams.

But Valente didn't get an answer. "No one is home," he said. "I don't think we should wait. I think we should move on. We need to get more distance between ourselves and Boss." He spoke first to Delfino in Spanish, then to the man in English.

Delfino remembered that Boss had said the camp must be kept secret—that he'd kill to keep it secret. So it was true that they had to get moving. But Delfino also knew they had to get help for Uncle José and the other men.

"We need to call the police," he said.

Valente was listening to the man, who said, "I better show you a back way to the railroad." He began to draw on a napkin. "You just go these dirt roads and come in on the back side of Mexican Hat. You'll hit the railroad tracks just past a big hay barn. Follow them railroad tracks. They'll take you into the flats. A heap of trains change in the flats. You hop that six o'clock train, and in five hours you'll roll into Houston."

Valente took the napkin and put it in his pocket.

Fear was pushing Delfino to leave, but he had to do something about the enslaved men. "What about calling the police?" he said again.

Valente translated.

The black man shook his head. "Not now. You don't have time to talk to cops now. Got to get some miles between you and that Boss man."

"We're worried about an old man in the camp who is sick," Valente told him.

"You can't do nothing about it now. And you can't do it down in South Texas anyway. You said that man has a lot of land. That means a lot of money. Probably pays off the police. No. You leave it to me. I'll study on it. Get those poor folks out of there some kind of way."

When Valente translated, Delfino knew the man must be right. He had thought of the police as the enemy because he was illegal. But until now he hadn't thought that they might work for Boss. Now a new fear chilled him.

"Can we do some work to pay for our meal? Some cleaning?" Valente asked the man.

"What are you talking about? You ain't got no time to mess around. You just get moving on down the road."

Valente extended his hand. "Thank you, Mr. . . ."

"Washington," the man said, taking Valente's hand. "My friends call me Wash." He shook hands with Delfino, too.

"Muchas gracias, señor. Muchas gracias."

They went to the door, and Salvador got up to let them out. He handed Wash the empty plate and bowl and said his thanks in Nahuatl.

"You just follow the tracks to Mexican Hat the way I showed you. If you need to, mention my name. Everybody knows Wash from Wings and Greens. My people know something about hiding from the man."

Valente put the pickax on his shoulder, and they were on their way.

Very soon they turned onto a dirt road. Their path seemed endless to Delfino. He was afraid for himself. He was worried about Uncle José. And Teresa. He was going farther and farther away from his sister. So much time had passed, and he had earned nothing to send Teresa. He didn't even know how she was.

He wondered if coming to the United States had been the right decision. So far, this had been a land of broken hopes, but it didn't have to stay that way. He still believed he could help Teresa. He might even help himself and find a place where he would be happy, as happy as . . .

Delfino searched his memories to find a happy one, but most of them were dark. He would be as happy as . . . he and Teresa were when they were children and ran away for the day. That was a good memory.

Delfino was supposed to watch the goats, and Teresa was supposed to be washing clothes. Instead, laughing, they slipped off together to play and enjoy the fine, mild day. A gentle breeze kissed their cheeks as they ran, their young legs hardly tiring. When they reached the wide meadow, they made themselves crowns of flowers and leaves and leaped about like goats, dizzy with freedom, despite the beating they knew their father would give them when they got home.

That had been a truly happy day. Remembering it, Delfino's steps grew lighter.

15

A Beating Heart

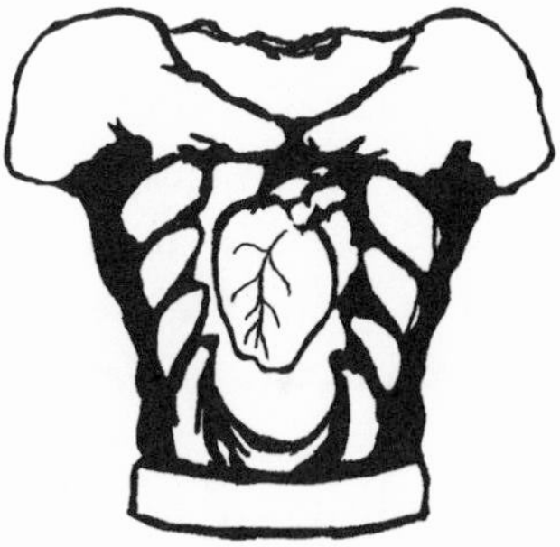

It was just daylight when they passed the big hay barn and came to the railroad tracks. Heartened by that success, the boys' spirits lifted with the dawn. Delfino thought of the dead Aztec warriors marching triumphantly with the rising sun and felt a surge of energy.

The boys eagerly followed the tracks, like tracing a river to its source. Delfino and Valente bounded along on the crossties, but Salvador and Bandit ran on the grassy ridge below. Delfino knew Salvador was protecting Bandit's feet from the rough gravel beside the tracks.

People were just beginning to stir when they got to the edge of Mexican Hat and to the area Wash had called the flats. It looked desolate. The buildings near the tracks were warehouses and some small homes. A few workers were arriving at the warehouses, and a few people were just leaving their homes. No one showed any interest in the boys and their dog. Delfino hoped that none of them would take it into their heads to call the Border Patrol, and he hoped none were connected with Boss. He knew he wouldn't feel easy until his feet touched Houston—if then.

The odor of coffee and frying bacon was in the air. The railroad tracks they were following converged with other tracks. Some boxcars waited there. The boys found one that was empty, hoisted Bandit in, and climbed in themselves.

"We have to close this door," Valente said.

"I don't like that idea," Delfino protested. "There is no way to open it from the inside. We need light and air. Maybe they won't even take this car." He would rather walk the whole way, however far, than be closed inside.

But Valente would not be persuaded. "Help me push," he insisted.

They pushed, and the heavy sliding door closed with a loud noise that made Delfino shudder. They were in to stay, for good or ill. The door couldn't be opened from the inside.

"Now huddle in the corner, and pray that nobody looks in."

"It's dark as the underworld in here," Delfino said softly, "I can't even see my hand."

The air felt heavy and stale, and there didn't seem to be enough of it. Delfino tried to imagine a gentle breeze.

You never know what to be thankful for until it's gone, he thought. I never expected to daydream about air.

"A whole boxcar full of illegals died one time," Valente said casually. "The railroad people were disinfecting the cars. They put some kind of gas in through the vent in the top, and the men all suffocated."[1]

"Nice story, Valente! What are you trying to do, scare me to death?"

"You don't need to be scared. We have our trusty pickax."

Delfino didn't translate for Salvador. He realized that more and more often he was not taking the trouble to include his cousin, but Valente's remarks didn't seem like something that needed to be repeated. It was tiresome to translate so much, and there were many things that Salvador wouldn't care about or understand. Still, Delfino felt another sheaf of guilt weighing on his shoulders. It didn't feel right leaving Salvador out.

At least he has Bandit, Delfino thought.

It was true. The bond between Salvador and the dog was as real as rope. They were bound together.

Delfino knew he was bound to Salvador, too. And to Teresa. They were all tied together with a rope that would never break.

Delfino remembered the rope Grandfather had given them. It was an old soft cotton one that wouldn't hurt their hands. They used to try to pull each other across a mark they had made in the dirt. That was a game Salvador always won. Delfino and Teresa pulled together with all their might, bracing their feet and straining, but Salvador would pull them both across the mark. They would all fall together in a pile, laughing.

Sometimes Grandfather would play the game with them. When he did, it was always the same. First, each child would be pulled across the line, caught in Grandfather's strong arms and tickled mercilessly. Then the children would band together, pulling with all their strength against Grandfather until at last, saying, "No, no I can't! Together you are too strong!" Grandfather would be pulled across the line, defeated, and tickled in his turn.

The boxcar jerked. Delfino left his memories and came back to the here and now. Metal clanked.

They were moving. Slowly.

Delfino realized that he was holding his breath. He held it until they picked up speed and were well under way. Then he propped himself in a corner. It seemed that he was hurtling between worlds, and he wondered what the new world would be like. The temperature wasn't high, but he was hot. Occasionally a jarring whistle sounded. The sound of the turning wheels lulled him, and he crossed the border into sleep.

He saw a headless torso floating across a grassy plain. It floated near the ground, seeming somehow earthbound even though it had no legs. It did not waft about aimlessly, borne by the wind, as Delfino would have expected. Rather, it moved purposefully,. as if it were intent on some task. Although headless, the torso seemed to be looking for something, or someone.

Delfino concealed himself behind a mesquite tree—the only tree on the broad plain. Terribly afraid, he stretched upward until he was long and thin as a reed, his legs wispy.

But the torso was not deceived. It came straight toward him. Its chest cavity opened and revealed a bleeding heart. He knew it was the dreadful Night Axe. The chest closed with a loud noise . . . opened, closed . . . opened, closed . . .[2]

Delfino knew what he must do. He must stand his ground. When the torso was near, he must thrust his hand into the open chest and snatch the beating heart before the ribs clanged shut again.

The torso came closer. And closer. Delfino raised his hand, ready to seize the bloody prize. His heart was pounding.

The torso floated within reach.

Delfino was ready, but his own heart was too loud. It beat in his ears. The sound of his heart wouldn't let him think.

Delfino turned and ran.

He raced across the desolate plain. There was no place to hide. No place to run, and he was absolutely by himself.

The pain of isolation was almost more than Delfino could bear. He felt himself hopelessly and forever alone. Nothing existed except boundless space and the grim torso that came calmly after him, intent on victory. All the while Delfino's heart sounded in his ears like ax blows.

"Hey, sleepyhead. Do you want to see daylight?"

Delfino awoke. A band of light streamed into the boxcar through a small opening. Valente swung the pickax, landed a firm blow, and the hole was still larger.[3]

The pounding ax sounds like my frightened heart, Delfino thought. I was hearing it as I dreamed.

Valente bent to look. "I think it's time to jump," he said. He stuck his arm through the hole and unfastened the boxcar door. "Okay, you guys, push it open."

"Come push, Salvador," Delfino said in Nahuatl. It felt good to have his cousin beside him. His dream was still with him. He could manage the fear—shrug it off even—but the awful isolation he had felt made him want to weep. As much as Delfino liked and needed Valente, at this moment it was Salvador's presence that comforted him. Salvador would stick with him forever. He was not alone.

They all pushed together, their hands flat against the sliding boxcar door. It opened enough for all four, boys and dog, to stand side by side. Light streamed into the heart of the boxcar.

Valente leaned out, steadying himself with one hand, and looked ahead. Delfino looked, too, though he wasn't sure what he was looking for. He could see a skyline ahead. The land was flat, but a grassy knoll came up to the railroad track.

Valente looked at Delfino and Salvador. "We have to make a wide jump onto the grass out there. Go one by one so we don't crash into each other."

Delfino translated for Salvador.

Salvador nodded and put his hand on Bandit's head.

"Are you ready, men?" Valente asked. But he didn't wait for an answer. He leaped out of the boxcar, springing in an arc like a deer.

Delfino followed. The fresh morning air surrounded him like a gentle sea, and he felt as if he were floating. To his left, he was aware of Salvador and of Bandit, arcing toward destiny.

Delfino landed, bounced, and rolled. He knew how to take a fall. They all did, except Bandit. Delfino wondered how the dog had fared.

From one side, he saw Valente walking toward him, a smile on his face. Delfino grinned back. Then, some yards away, he saw Salvador, sitting easily with one knee bent and one leg stretched in front of him, speaking to Bandit, who was panting happy pants.

I guess the jump didn't jar Bandit too much, Delfino thought. He seems as glad to be here as we are.

"Come on, Red Dog Tlashtehqui," he called in Nahuatl. "Lead us on through the underworld."

Delfino felt his heart pounding. He remembered his dream and laid his hand on his chest.

16

Delfino's First Dollar

The three boys fell into step with Bandit trotting a little ahead.

"Another road, another adventure," Valente said, cheerful as always.

"I'd just as soon not have any more adventures," Delfino answered. "What I want is a plain, dull life, with each day just the same as the day before—safe."

He was tired of always looking over his shoulder. Even now, when they had barely reached Houston, Delfino watched for Boss. He couldn't know where they were, but he would try to track them down. And Delfino remembered that Boss was supposed to meet Pino in Houston.

The land had changed. At the slave camp, there had been desert and hardscrabble earth. There the sun's rays struck you like arrows. Here everything was green. Trees were abundant. So were the grass and other plants. The air was damp, and the sky was overcast. Delfino felt closed in, trapped by the heavy clouds.

The city was strange. It was open and clean, but it felt empty. He had expected crowded streets like in Mexico City, with people walking, horns honking, vendors on the corners, and *muchachos* running about. But here the cars didn't honk. No one walked on the streets. The houses lay isolated in green yards. Three boys and a dog on foot stood out. How could they hide?

Delfino saw yellow arches. He gasped and clutched his chest. It was the same café that Boss had taken them to! How could that be?

Valente laughed when Delfino told him what was wrong. But Valente's laugh wasn't mocking. It was the reassuring laugh of a friend. "There are a million of those in the States! Don't worry!"

They came to a parking lot crowded with cars. There was a big store in the middle of the lot. The sign said *El Mercado,* and people were pushing baskets of groceries to their cars.

"Let's help some of these women load their sacks. That's a way to earn tips," Valente said.

Delfino nodded and started to translate for Salvador, but Valente interrupted. "He'd better stay back with the dog. The women might be frightened."

"Stay here with Bandit," Delfino told Salvador. "He might startle people."

Delfino wasn't sure that Valente was referring only to Bandit. Maybe he was, but he also seemed to mean that Salvador would frighten people. Delfino felt a flash of anger—toward Valente and toward the women with their full grocery bags and their fat babies.

He swallowed his anger.

"We won't be long," he told Salvador in Nahuatl. "Be patient."

Delfino meant the last words as a joke because they were the ones Salvador always said to him—the lesson he, not Salvador, was learning—but Salvador didn't realize Delfino was joking. He nodded agreeably, his eyes in some other world.

"We may frighten people ourselves," Delfino told Valente. "We look like cavemen."

"Use your smile, and tell them their babies are cute," Valente answered. He trotted toward a woman who was opening the trunk of her car.

"*Señora,* let me help you." Valente had one of the woman's grocery bags in his arms before she could reply. He smiled as he put it in the trunk and picked up another. The woman smiled back and opened her purse.

She's getting out his tip, Delfino thought. Watching Valente is a good lesson. A *campesino* like me can learn a lot from a city person like him.

Delfino felt awkward, but he pushed his feelings down deep where he wouldn't notice them and hurried over to a woman with a full grocery cart. *"Señora, con permiso."*

The woman had a kind face. One part of Delfino wanted to tell her about the slave camp and ask her for help, but he couldn't risk that. They had to find help without getting themselves sent back across the border.

Delfino thanked the woman for the tip and moved on.

In an hour, Delfino and Valente each had a handful of change. Delfino felt a sense of satisfaction. He had earned his first American money.

"Now I can call my brother. Then we're going to have ourselves some tacos," Valente said.

Delfino was just as glad to hear the brother mentioned as he had been when they were in Wings and Greens. Maybe this time Valente's brother would be home.

An outdoor pay phone was nearby. Delfino and Salvador stood just out of earshot. Delfino wanted to give Valente privacy, but he couldn't make himself look away.

He watched eagerly—watched Valente's fingers drop the coins and punch the numbers, watched the set of his body as he waited for an answer and the slight movement forward of his shoulders as he spoke. His body relaxed, and his head made little animated movements as he talked. Then he stiffened and took a small step backwards. Something was wrong.

Valente spoke energetically. He gestured with his free hand. His shoulders lifted and fell as with a sigh, then slumped forward as he hung up the phone. He kicked a can as he came back toward Delfino and Salvador.

"What's wrong?" Delfino asked.

Valente punched the air with his fist. He stamped his foot and punched the air again, as if he couldn't answer until he got rid of some anger.

"My brother went on a drunk, and his boss is mad. He can't come."

Delfino was stunned.

"He's messed up so bad, he probably couldn't get me work anyway."

Delfino drew a deep breath. Another dream had crumbled, and time was running out. Teresa would be five months along by now. He had to find work fast.

Valente muttered angrily. "Stupid. Stupid. Stupid." He punched the air again and again. "Stupid. Stupid."

Salvador and Bandit stood together quietly. Salvador's hand rested lightly on Bandit's head. Bandit watched Valente intently, his eyes bright and his expression alert. The dog seemed more aware of what was happening than Salvador, whose familiar mild, vague expression did not change.

Delfino explained what had happened. Salvador nodded calmly.

At least I never have to worry that Salvador will be angry or complain, Delfino thought. He wasn't sure whether Salvador's calmness was because he was strange or whether it was because his Aztec nature, purer than Delfino's own, made him accept fate. Whatever the reason, Delfino was grateful. He drew strength from his cousin.

"Didn't I hear you mention tacos?" he said to Valente with a smile. He wanted to lighten the mood and give Valente the kind of cheerful boost Valente had so often given him. "After we eat some meat, we can handle anything."

Valente grinned back at Delfino. It was a crooked grin, but it was a start. "You're right, *amigo,*" he said. "Let's eat." His voice was a little shaky.

They went into the grocery store, and again Salvador stayed outside with Bandit. Delfino didn't like leaving his cousin, but anything might happen if they left Bandit alone with all those people coming and going.

It's Salvador's own fault, Delfino thought. He wouldn't even leave the slave camp without the dog.

Somehow that didn't make Delfino feel any better.

There were mountains of fruit and vegetables, and there were aisles and aisles of canned food in the store. A lively tune was playing. It was all splendid, but Delfino felt tense. He expected to see Boss in every aisle he passed.

A Mexican woman stood behind a lunch counter frying ground meat. Delfino handed Valente his money and sank onto a stool. The spicy aroma of the rich food had made him weak.

Valente didn't seem weak. He hadn't even sat down. His sturdy, lithe body fidgeted as he waited for their order.

"I don't need my brother," he told Delfino, sounding like his old confident self again. "I know how to get along without him. Especially with two good pals and a big dog to help."

Delfino knew that Valente was just trying to make himself feel better, but he seemed to be doing a good job of it. Valente never stayed down for long.

Delfino rested his arm on the counter. He noticed how thin and bony it looked.

A man is supposed to be meat and bone, *carne y hueso,* but I'm just bones. If I had more meat covering them like Valente and Salvador do, maybe I wouldn't wear out so fast, Delfino thought. He had always been thin, and Teresa even thinner. He thought how important it was for her to gain some weight and strength before the baby came.

"Do you know where we could pick up some work?" Valente asked the woman who was preparing their order.

"Maybe right behind this store," she answered. "A man from produce told me some trucks got here early. You might get work helping them unload."

Valente and Delfino didn't wait. They took their food and turned to go.

"Ask for Feliciano," the woman said as they left. "He does the hiring."

They hurried out, eating as they went and carrying food for Salvador and Bandit.

The man named Feliciano was talking to one of the truck drivers, a rumpled, brawny fellow who kept wiping his face with a bandanna. Feliciano himself was as thin and erect as a flagpole and just as neat. His white shirt was crisp. His dark blue pants were sharply creased, and he wore a tie that exactly matched the pants. His skin had the glow of perfect health. Even when he was standing in conversation, you could see that he was quick and energetic, and he had a happy, smiling face that matched his name—Feliciano, the joyful one.

Delfino could hardly believe finding work was so easy. Feliciano smiled as he showed them what to do. They had to unload bananas, potatoes, and lettuce from three produce trucks. Bandit lay in the shade under one of them. No one cared or even seemed to notice.

The workers seemed friendly enough, and spoke Spanish. There was only one unpleasant incident. Feliciano fired a man. He was a young, dull-eyed Mexican-American with a gold chain around his neck. His name was Martin Gonzales. Feliciano heard him talking to another worker and got so angry he fired him on the spot. "Take your two-bit protection racket and get out of here," Feliciano told him. "I don't want your foot on this lot again."

Martin swore a string of oaths, then shouted, "You better be careful what you say to me. My uncle works for Pino."

"Pino doesn't know you're alive, and he could be your brother for all I care. Get out of here." Feliciano's face, which had been so radiant and smiling, was sharp as an ax blade.

The name Pino fell like a blow on Delfino's ears.

They worked more than four hours. Delfino was glad when they finished. He didn't think he could have gone on much longer. He noticed that Valente's strength was lagging, too.

Only Salvador seemed as strong as ever—as strong as when they left Mexico.

Feliciano smiled radiantly and gave each of them twenty dollars.

"Do you know a place where we could stay tonight?" Valente asked.

"Just down this road are some apartments. A lot of men without papers stay there. You can probably stay with some of them."

"How about work? Will you have more for us tomorrow?"

"I can use one man. This one." He indicated Salvador.

Delfino said, "My cousin doesn't speak Spanish . . . or English."

Feliciano shrugged. "I'm not hiring him to talk. I'm hiring him to lift."

Delfino told Salvador in Nahuatl.

Then he asked Feliciano, "Can't you use me, too?"

But Feliciano shook his head. He picked up a banana that had been tossed into a pile of damaged fruit, broke off the bruised end, and took a bite of the good half. "You can take any of this stuff you want, though. We all do. Then the night people throw it away."

Por Dios, this really is the Promised Land, Delfino thought. He lifted his gaze. Among the cars passing on the street was a white pickup. His heart sank. "Valente, look!"

"*Hombre*, that's not Boss!" Valente said. He grasped Delfino's shoulder to reassure him. "There are a lot of white pickups in the world. Look—there's not a dent or a red smudge on the fender, and the license tag doesn't say BOSS-1."

Valente was right. Delfino drew a deep breath of relief.

If I keep this up, Boss won't need to kill me, he thought. I'll die of heart failure before I'm seventeen.

17

A Swarm of Bees

When they reached the apartments, a number of people were in the courtyard. It was almost like a little village in Mexico. Children ran and played. Mexican music sounded from apartment and car windows. People came in and out in a steady flow —women and children, old men, grandmothers. Martin Gonzales, the fellow Feliciano fired, was in a group of young men who lounged against some cars, smoking.

Another group of men were illegals. It was easy to spot the people who were from the other side of the border—*los del otro lado*—or at least the ones who were newly arrived. Their shoes, their clothes, but most of all their expressions gave them away. Delfino saw Martin speak to a thin, tired-looking illegal who handed him something.

People always say that the immigration, the *immi,* can smell out illegals, Delfino thought, but that's not right. They don't need to take a single sniff—one glance is enough. Do I look like them—so desperate and so hollow? Is my skin dull like theirs?

Delfino remembered the image that had looked back at him from the mirror in Wings and Greens. He didn't like to remember that fierce, hard face. I'm not going to stay like that. I want to glow like Feliciano.

They didn't have any trouble finding some other illegals who would share their lodging and who needed money badly enough to let Bandit stay, too—for a while at least.

Altogether there were ten men in the apartment. There wasn't much furniture, just a couple of old chairs someone had found. There were a few dishes and pans in the kitchen, and a radio that stayed on night and day. All the men slept on the floor. Some of them had pillows.

"Better the floor here than a cot at the farm," Delfino remarked.

"You said it," Valente answered. "Any old corner looks good to me. I'm ready for dreamland."

Salvador's vague, placid face was anxious. "We have to talk to the police about the farm," he told Delfino. "We have to help Uncle José. We have to help Lamb."

"You're right," Delfino answered. "We will."

The trouble was he didn't know how to help them, and he was terribly frightened. If he went to the police they would send him and Salvador back to Mexico. Worse, even here in Houston the police might know Boss. After all, he sent trucks here. He might be paying the police to be quiet or even to help him. Delfino knew he and Salvador could get themselves and Valente killed.

"We can't really talk to the police," Delfino explained to Salvador. "It's too dangerous. We'll write a letter."

Delfino went back to El Mercado and bought a tablet, a pencil, and a package of envelopes. As he returned to the apartment, a figure stepped out of the shadows and blocked his way. It was Martin Gonzales. His gold chain gleamed, and he looked down at Delfino threateningly.

"*Mojado*, I'm a businessman. I give protection to wetbacks. I don't charge much—just part of your pay every week."

"I'm not giving you my money!" Delfino said. He was exhausted, but he was ready to fight even for the change in his pocket.

Martin smiled confidently. "People who don't pay get picked up by the *immi.* It just takes one phone call, but I'll give you a few days before I collect. I'm a reasonable man." He stepped back into the shadows and was gone.

Shaken, Delfino hurried to the apartment. He didn't tell Salvador what had happened. Instead, he sat against the wall with the tablet on his knees and Salvador beside him.

He tried to write, but couldn't think what to say, and Martin Gonzales kept popping into his head. His brain just wouldn't work. He struggled to find the right words, but fell asleep, jerking awake as his head fell forward. "Cousin, I'm sorry. I can't write the letter now. I'll write it tomorrow."

Salvador nodded.

Delfino wondered where he should send the letter when he got it written. Valente would know, he decided. Valente could write one, too, in English. Then Delfino sank into sleep and found himself back at the slave camp.

He was breaking bone-colored rocks. He looked for Salvador and Valente, but he was alone. In the distance, he saw a small dark cloud approaching. It buzzed as it came closer. It was bees. Something told him they were killer bees. He knew a man had no chance against a swarm of killer bees. His blood chilled so sharply that he could feel his veins like a maze in his body.

Then Delfino realized he was running. But he couldn't outrun the bees. Their hum grew louder. There was nowhere to hide, no pond or stream to keep him safe from their ferocious stings. He flung his arms madly, stumbling and sliding as he ran. At last, he covered his face with his hands and rushed blindly through rocks and thorns. The buzz gnashed and rattled like bones grinding together.

"Mictlantecuhtli! Mictlantecuhtli! Mictlantecuhtli!"

Delfino screamed in horror and despair. Not bees but a swarm of skulls was upon him, clattering the name of the god of the underworld.

"Mictlantecuhtli! Mictlantecuhtli! Mictlantecuhtli!"

Delfino tripped and fell. The ground fell away beneath him.

He awoke, sweating and cold.

He saw Salvador sitting with the tablet on his knee. That's strange, Delfino thought. Salvador can't read or write. He felt weak from the dream. Sleep washed over him again.

The next day, Delfino insisted that he and Valente write the letters before they even went out to look for jobs. Valente wrote his letter quickly, but Delfino was slow with pen and paper. His eyes itched, and his head ached. Whenever he closed his eyes, he saw a skull or the skeleton in the cave.

"We'll send these to the Houston Police Department," Valente told him. He addressed the envelopes, and they went by a post office on their way to look for work. They stopped at a pay phone, too, and Delfino called home.

In Ahuelican, there was one telephone. It was in a house in the center of the village, a kind of community center. Delfino knew that Teresa wouldn't be there, but someone would. He left a message saying exactly when he would call back. He picked a time a week away so he would be sure to have money. Then at last they were off to find work, walking together, and Delfino told Valente about Martin Gonzales.

Valente gave a low whistle. "We can't get mixed up with anything Pino touches," he said, "but I don't believe this Martin Gonzales. Anybody who was really with Pino would keep his mouth shut about it."

"Why? Who is this Pino?"

"He's a crook. A big one. He's vicious, and he's powerful on both sides of the border. But just because Martin Gonzales mentions his name doesn't mean we'll give him money."

Delfino felt relieved. He was glad to have Valente to rely on. He didn't know anything about that kind of stuff, or about how to find a job either. Valente's experience in the States was a big help. We'll find work fast, he thought.

But things didn't turn out that way.

Too young. Too small. Those were words Delfino got used to hearing.

Valente got a job with a yard service, but they wouldn't take Delfino.

"I'm not too small to push a lawnmower," he pleaded.

The man in charge shook his head. "I don't know how old you really are," he said, "but even if you were twenty, I wouldn't hire you. You look about fourteen."

Delfino felt himself flush with anger and embarrassment. I wish I weren't so little and scrawny, he thought. If I were bigger, I could make money for Teresa.

His anxiety about his sister was a constant pain that never left him. He sometimes felt his vitals gripping the pain, doubling around it like a fist gripping a stone. Teresa had always helped him. Now he couldn't help her.

Delfino remembered one day when he had left the goats to graze by themselves and had slipped off to school. He often left his work to go to the school, and each time he paid for it with a beating. But that time was worse than usual.

His father had come to the school in a drunken rage. Teresa ran behind him. He dragged Delfino out and began beating him very hard with a strong stick. Teresa tugged at their father, but he wouldn't stop. Finally she pushed herself between Delfino and their father and took a dreadful blow, right in the face. The blood flowed. It shocked their father, who turned and went home.

Teresa still carried a scar on her right cheek. Delfino could never forget what she had done. He had to make money for her.

He went back to talk to Feliciano. "Don't you have something for me? I'm a hard worker."

"I'll remember you," Feliciano told him, smiling his great joyful smile. "When I have work, I'll remember you."

Delfino was sure Feliciano meant what he said, but he had a hard time making himself smile back at him. It was disheartening to be told *no* day after day, and to have to live looking over his shoulder. Every time he saw Martin Gonzales, he felt nervous. More than once, he'd been sure he glimpsed Boss's pickup.

He felt that he should look for work in other parts of the city, but the buses were slow, and the city was enormous. Many areas turned out to be just office buildings or houses, and he didn't know who to ask for work. It was too confusing. And every time he saw yellow arches, his old fear fell on him like a dark shadow. He missed having Valente to guide him and laugh shadows away, but Valente worked long hours now.

By day Delfino wandered the city like a ghost. By night he was pursued by swarms of skulls.

18

A Little Crumb

Delfino began standing every morning at a corner with other men who wanted work. People who needed stoop labor for the day came there. There were always many more men than there were jobs, and people hired the bigger, stronger men.

I'm quick, Delfino thought. Quick and smart. Can't they see that? But Delfino found himself left behind with Bandit while Salvador and Valente went to work. He kept writing letters, but he was afraid to sign his name or put his address. He didn't know if the letters were being taken seriously, or if they were even being read. He felt frustrated and helpless. He asked Valente to think of other places to write, so Valente asked veiled questions when he was at work. Later he told Delfino he could write to the Immigration Service itself and to the FBI.

Delfino did. He spent a long morning writing each letter. Valente looked up the addresses in the phone book and wrote them on the envelopes.

Sometimes Delfino hustled tips at the grocery store. Sometimes he and Bandit took long walks. "We got so used to walking, we can't quit, eh Bandit?" he joked one afternoon as they crossed the courtyard.

"You talk to your dog like a person," a small voice said in Spanish.

Delfino couldn't see where the voice came from for a moment. Then he saw a little boy, perhaps five years old, sitting under the stairs.

"Well, Tlashcaltzintli, that's because he *is* a person," Delfino answered kindly, using Grandfather's word for a small child—Bread Crumb. "Come out of there and meet him."

The boy came out slowly, his steps hesitant.

"That's right," Delfino said to encourage him. "Come on. See, I'm between you and the dog."

The boy inched forward, then took a couple of quick steps and grabbed Delfino's leg. He was no taller than Bandit. They looked directly into each other's eyes. Delfino felt the boy's arms tighten on his leg. He was moved by the child's trusting grasp.

I don't blame Bread Crumb for being afraid, Delfino thought. Big red Bandit is scary to anyone, much less to a little Crumb like this.

"Tlashcaltzintli, this is Tlashtehqui. You are sure to be good friends; your names are alike."

The boy was very tiny. Now Delfino remembered seeing him before. "Come on, Tzintli," he said. "Let's sit over here in the shade. I'll tell you a story."

They sat on the curb. Bandit and the boy both looked at Delfino expectantly. He wouldn't disappoint them. He remembered Grandfather's stories.

He spoke calmly and seriously.

"A long time ago the supreme god sent for a human pair. They were Tata and his wife, Nena.[1] When they stood before the supreme god, he told them that a fierce flood would soon come. It would destroy everything that lay in its course. The supreme god said that Tata and Nena could save themselves by making a hole in a great tree and hiding in it, but he warned them that they must not be greedy. He told them they must not eat more than one ear of corn each.

"Tata and Nena made a hole in a great tree as they were told. When the flood came, they were ready. They stayed in the hole and were safe, but the flood lasted a long time and they were hungry.

"When the water went down, they climbed out. As soon as their feet touched the earth, they saw a fish. They remembered what the supreme god had told them, but they were so hungry they caught the fish and built a fire to cook it, anyway. Smoke from their fire rose into the air and wafted to the nose of the supreme god.

"The god was angry. He was so angry that he turned Tata and Nena into dogs."

Delfino made a gesture with his hands to show that the story was over. "Now, Bread Crumb, you see why I said Bandit is a person and why I treat him like one."

Bandit was panting happily, as if he had understood.

The little boy was solemn. "They were hungry," he said. "The god wasn't fair." He reached out and touched Bandit gently as if to comfort him.

Bandit moved closer. He rested his jaw on the child's shoulder and put his nose against the child's neck. They stood perfectly still. Delfino knew the boy and the dog were now fast friends. But the child's words raised a troubling question—a question Delfino had broken his head over many times. Why was everything so unfair? Could there possibly be a just god?

Delfino shook his head as if to jar those thoughts out. He preferred to be happy about his charming new friend. "Come on," he said, "I'll buy you a hot ear of corn at El Mercado Grocery Store."

Delfino knew that was a frivolity. He shouldn't spend money so carelessly, but he felt expansive. Besides, it was almost time for Salvador to get off work. They could walk back with him. He would enjoy meeting this little Bread Crumb. Delfino hoped Teresa would have a bright, winsome child like Bread Crumb.

Days passed. Salvador's work turned out to be steady, and there was the bonus of discarded fruit and vegetables. He brought home enough for them to share with Bread Crumb's parents—his hardworking young father, Juan, and his smiling young mother, Maria. Her stomach was swelling with a second child. Delfino was glad they had fruit and vegetables to share. He never looked at Maria without thinking of Teresa and thinking that she needed fresh food, too. He *had* to earn some money.

On Salvador's first day off, Delfino swallowed his pride and asked his cousin to go with him to the corner where laborers waited, hoping for work.

"Maybe someone will pick you, and I can come, too. I'll tell them we are together. Then if I can prove myself, they might let me work again."

Salvador had made enough money for each of them to buy a shirt and a pair of pants. And they each had a new haircut. Delfino hadn't wanted to spend a cent on those things, but Valente insisted. "If you look bad, no one will hire you," he said, and Delfino had known he was right.

"We don't look like wild men any more," Delfino said jokingly as he and Salvador were about to leave the apartment. "When we first got here, people were probably more afraid of our bites than of Bandit's."

The dog heard his name and came wagging, ready to go out.

"Not this time," Delfino told him. "You have to stay here."

Salvador looked into the courtyard. "Our little Tzintli is out there. He can bring Bandit back if we get a job." So Bandit and Bread Crumb came along.

The men waiting on the corner shrank back from the dog, even though the child had his arm around his neck.

"Move away from Bandit if a car pulls up," Delfino told Salvador. "We don't want people to think we intend to bring him along to work."

No car came for a long time. At last a van pulled up. Two men got out.

"Immigration!" they said.

"La migra," someone echoed.

The men scattered in all directions.

"Come on, Salvador! Run!" Delfino said in Nahuatl. His thin legs were already in motion.

Delfino had run more than a block when he looked back over his shoulder and gasped. Salvador wasn't with him. Had the immigration picked him up?

Worried, Delfino sneaked back toward the corner and peeped from behind a parked car. Several of the illegals had been caught and were in the van. The others—the quick, lucky ones like Delfino—had disappeared. But Salvador, Bandit, and Bread Crumb still stood calmly in the same place.

As the immigration van drove off, Bread Crumb lifted his hand and waved farewell. The man behind the wheel waved in response.

Delfino was puzzled. The man seemed friendly. Why hadn't he bothered Salvador? Was it because of the child beside him? Perhaps they wouldn't want to leave a child there alone. Or maybe it was because of Bandit. Maybe they were afraid of him. Or maybe they were put off by Salvador's vague expression and those other-world eyes. Or was it destiny at work? Maybe Salvador's *tonali* had protected him.

Whatever the reason, they were safe for now. Delfino waited until the van was well out of sight before he joined them.

19

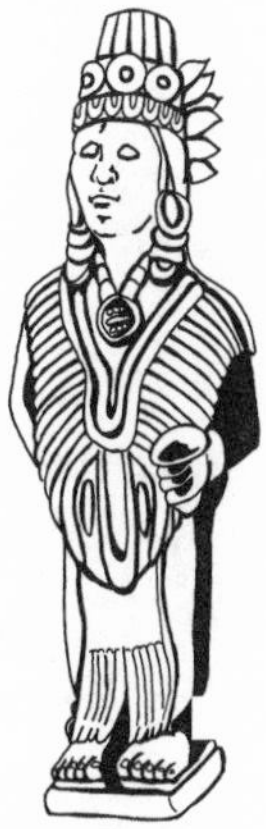

The Remarkable Bitsy Clay

"What happened?" Delfino asked.

"Some men came and took some other men with them," Salvador answered. "They patted Tzintli on the head."

"I spoke to them in English," Bread Crumb told Delfino. "I said, 'Don't bother my Daddy. My Daddy isn't illegal.'" He laughed out loud, proud of himself.

Delfino laughed, too. Saved by a child, he thought, and by Salvador's calmness, too. He's not scared, so he's safe.

Delfino and Salvador made their phone call to the village that evening, but instead of being reassured, Delfino was more anxious than ever. Teresa's light voice came over the wires with her familiar intonation, but without her normal liveliness.

"I'm fine," she told him. "The baby is kicking me. It's a strong baby."

Something told Delfino that Teresa was just trying to make him feel better and to keep up her spirits. "Sister, may I speak to your husband?" he asked.

Melchor came on the line.

"Tell me the truth," Delfino said. "How is Teresa?"

"She is not very strong," Melchor answered. "I am beginning to think you and Padre Ignacio are right, and my family is wrong. I want to take her to a doctor, but I won't have any money until we harvest the corn."

"We'll send you money every week," Delfino said. "At least there will be enough to get her good food. She needs meat and milk."

Delfino tried even harder to find work, but no one would hire him. He tried not to give in to hopelessness, but it was hard for him to keep trying and never have any success. It was hard to keep believing in himself. He began to feel small and dependent —another Bread Crumb. And he still worried about Martin Gonzales. What if Valente was wrong?

Salvador worked for Feliciano almost every day, so there was money for them to eat and to pay their share of the rent, but there wasn't much left to send to Mexico—not nearly as much as Delfino wanted to send—and Salvador had earned it all. Delfino had to depend on his cousin.

Grandfather had taught them to stay close together. "Two sticks are harder to break than one," he always said. So Delfino's bad feelings weren't because he couldn't lean on his cousin freely, but because he had always thought of himself as the bright one, the bold one, the leader. Things were different now. The tables had turned.

Finally, Delfino didn't know where to look for work any more. He slept more, but he was haunted by dreams. It was hard for him to act cheerful. Several times in the night, he saw Salvador sitting with his back against the wall, a tablet on his knees.

Salvador often left for work in the mornings before Delfino was out of bed. One day he returned to the apartment in midmorning, breathing deeply. He had run all the way, and he spoke louder than usual to be heard over the radio that was blasting *las noticias*, the news. "Come on, Cousin. Feliciano wants you."

Delfino rolled over and looked up curiously. "What does he want?" he asked, realizing as he spoke that Salvador couldn't possibly know what Feliciano wanted. Feliciano didn't speak Nahuatl.

"He said your name and motioned for me to fetch you. There's a lady there. A skinny white lady."

Delfino washed his face and combed his hair carefully. He and Salvador jogged back to El Mercado with Bandit beside them.

A small thin woman was standing in the sunlight near the loading dock behind the store, talking to Feliciano. Her skin was leathery, sunburned to a deep brown, and deeply wrinkled. Her eyes were bright blue, and her tousled hair was the color of salt and pepper. She wore a faded red shirt, faded blue jeans, and worn cowboy boots, but Delfino knew she wasn't poor. She seemed too sure of herself for that. Something about the way she stood told him that she was used to having her own way.

"This is Delfino," Feliciano said in Spanish in his smiling, gracious way. "I'm sure the two of you will get along very well."

"Soy Bitsy," she said as she stuck out her hand. *"Soy la señora* Bitsy Clay."

Delfino shook her hand, feeling shy, but reassured by her friendly manner and because she spoke Spanish.

"And who is this?" she asked, moving briskly toward Bandit who had lain down by a truck. "Hello there, Honey Dog," she said to Bandit, stretching her hand toward him—to pat him or to be sniffed, Delfino didn't know which.

He moved to get between her and the dog. Bandit had learned to be gentle with people he knew, but this woman was a stranger and her movements were too quick.

Salvador had gone back to work carrying produce into the store, but he appeared from behind some crates and jumped down from the loading dock. He spoke the dog's name. "Tlashtehqui."

"Señora, be careful!" Feliciano exclaimed. "That's a *perro bravo."*

"Oh, nonsense," Bitsy said. Then she addressed the dog again. "What's the matter with these old boys, Honey Dog?" It was easy to understand *la señora* even though she had a funny accent.

Salvador spoke to the dog softly in Nahuatl.

Bitsy let Bandit sniff her hand, then scratched him behind the ears and under the chin. "These fellows make a fuss over nothing, don't they, Honey Boy?"

"*Señora*, this is my cousin Salvador," Delfino said. "It's his dog."

Bitsy shook Salvador's hand. She looked at him with frank blue eyes and did not seem in the least bothered by his vague gaze. "You have a wonderful dog."

To Delfino she said, "Okay, Sonny. *Vámonos.*"

Delfino was struck by her easy familiarity. She seemed to think that everyone was her friend and that there were no dangers in the world for her. He followed her to her car—a big white Cadillac. Three young Mexican men waited beside it.

"Let's get going," she said.

The memory of how unsuspecting he had been with Boss made Delfino pause. He could get trapped in another slave camp. Delfino pushed that thought from his mind. He had to go.

La señora Bitsy moved her big purse from the seat to the floorboard, and Delfino got in the front seat. He looked over at her apprehensively. Then all his fears dropped away. This skinny graying woman with leathery skin and a big grin just wasn't scary. Delfino decided to enjoy his ride in the big, plush car.

When they got out of the city and on the highway, *la señora* Bitsy Clay put the radio on a Spanish-language station. Occasionally she sang along with a song. She got the words right, but she got the notes wrong. Delfino tried not to smile. He didn't want *la señora* Bitsy to think he was laughing at her, although he didn't really believe she would care. She seemed completely happy with herself and with the world.

They had driven almost an hour when they pulled into a long, tree-lined driveway that led to a big, elegant house. It was tall and of red brick. The lawns were so wide, it seemed to Delfino that there was enough space for a whole village. Several other cars were in the parking area, and there were two smaller houses behind the great house.

This looks like something in a movie, Delfino thought. I never expected to be at a place like this.

"Okay, men. It's time to dig." Bitsy spoke cheerfully as they got out of the car.

She showed them three huge oak stumps. "We lost these trees in a storm a few weeks ago," she said, sounding regretful. "We got them all cut and carried off except for these stumps."

That must have been the same storm we ran away in, Delfino thought.

"Restroom's over there." Bitsy pointed to a door at the back of a garage. She gave each of the workers a shovel and put two axes nearby. "Go for it," she said. Then, without further instruction, she left.

The workers all looked at each other, dumbfounded. Then they laughed.

"*Soy* Delfino," Delfino said.

"Fernando."

"Francisco."

"Javier."

They were all young. All illegal. And all eager.

"Let's see if we can do what this funny lady wants," Delfino said. They began digging in a fury of energy.

Soon Bitsy brought a pitcher of iced water and placed it nearby. Then they didn't see her for two or three hours, when she called to them.

"Wash up. It's time to eat." She motioned that they were to come to the house.

They went one by one to the garage restroom. Delfino was last. He scrubbed his hands, arms, and face carefully, and he dampened and smoothed his hair. When he finished, the others were already on the screened veranda. They stood shyly beside a table laden with food.

Bitsy looked out the door. "Good heavens, why are you standing there? Help yourselves. Eat." Then she disappeared again.

There were several kinds of meat and several kinds of cheese. There was white bread and brown bread. Mustard. Mayonnaise. Lettuce. Corn chips. Potato chips. And there was a big bowl of fruit—apples, oranges, bananas, pears.

They loaded their plates and sat awkwardly at a glass-topped table.

"We've gone to paradise," Delfino said, "and the head angel is named Bitsy Clay."

The others laughed and began eating at full speed. But Delfino didn't think he had made a good joke. It's more truth than joke, he thought.

He sat back in his chair and looked across the beautiful grounds. What lay before him looked better than any heaven he had ever heard of—Aztec or Christian. He looked back toward the tree stumps. They would finish digging them today, but maybe they would need to split them and carry them somewhere, too. Maybe they could come back tomorrow.

My life has been full of bad days, he thought, but a solitary good day sometimes comes along—even two good days. Once in a while, there is a miracle.

Even as Delfino congratulated himself on his happiness, anxiety weighed on him. He kept thinking about Uncle José stumbling along the rows, too exhausted to walk, much less work. Writing letters was not enough. Delfino wanted to do more, but he couldn't think what to do. Salvador was worried, too. He nodded whenever Delfino told him he had written another letter, but Delfino could see that he wasn't satisfied. And Martin Gonzales would be back. Delfino knew that some of the men were paying him, but he was resolved not to. Teresa needed money.

When Delfino saw Bitsy again, she had on a black dress, high heels, and earrings, but she carried the same big purse. Her graying hair was carefully arranged.

"Put up the tools and come on," she called. "I've got to go."

They zoomed down the highway. Bitsy was in a hurry, but she was in a good mood. She muttered happily to herself all the way to Houston. Occasionally she glanced at a piece of paper. Delfino decided she was practicing a declamation or a speech.

La señora Bitsy barely pulled over to the curb in front of the grocery store. "Jump out," she said, handing them each some bills. "I'll get you tomorrow. Eight o'clock. Same place." And she was gone.

Delfino and the other boys stood on the sidewalk, still a little stunned by the remarkable Bitsy Clay. Then they counted their money. Forty dollars! They each had forty dollars.

Delfino had earned his first day's wages and there would be more tomorrow. He felt like dancing, but he forced himself to walk normally—almost.

He remembered that Grandfather had said a man should always move sedately and with dignity. Delfino chanted the rules to himself: "Don't throw your feet or raise them too high, or you will be named a fool. Don't go bustling or strutting around. Don't act like a firefly."[1]

They were good rules, but Delfino couldn't resist an occasional exuberant skip. The crowded parking lot with its cars and grocery carts, with its darting children, its slow-moving old people, its mothers and babies—they all seemed like part of a great festival to him now, and all the people seemed to be celebrating life. The tinkling sound of the children's ride in front of the store was glorious music.

A voice in Delfino's head sang, "The Promised Land. The Promised Land. I've reached the Promised Land."

20

Grandfather Remembered

Over at the edge of the parking lot, Delfino saw Salvador and a man in uniform—a policeman. He ran toward them, his mouth dry with fear. Had Martin Gonzales turned them in?

The policeman, a big young man with blue eyes and a puzzled expression, was looking at a tablet Salvador was showing him. Bandit lay watchfully a few feet away.

That's the tablet he's been marking on in the night, Delfino thought. Martin Gonzales hadn't turned them in, after all.

"Please excuse my cousin," he said to the policeman in Spanish. "He doesn't understand very much."

The policeman shook his head. *"No hablo español,"* he answered in a flat, heavy accent. He turned and beckoned for someone to come, calling "Arturo!"

Salvador kept pointing to the tablet. He knew no one would understand his Nahuatl. When the officer looked away, Salvador pulled at his sleeve insistently and pointed again.

"Come on, Salvador, let's go," Delfino said, putting his hand on his cousin's back and giving him a little push.

Bandit trotted over beside Salvador.

"What do you mean talking to the police?" Delfino tried to say calmly. "You'll get us in trouble."

"I have to," Salvador answered.

The second policeman—Arturo—joined them, and the first policeman spoke to him as he gestured toward Salvador and the tablet.

"What's the matter?" Arturo asked Salvador in Spanish. Bandit was sitting quietly beside him.

Still silent, Salvador pointed to the tablet. Then he turned a page and pointed again. Delfino couldn't see what he was showing them, but he had an idea what it must be.

All the good things I've finally found are about to be taken away from me, Delfino thought. We're going to get sent back to Mexico.

Delfino trembled, but he tried to hold his voice steady as he spoke to Officer Arturo in Spanish. "Sir, my cousin is simple-minded. He doesn't mean anything."

"Hmm." Arturo took the tablet from Salvador and looked at it carefully. Then he shrugged. "You drew some nice pictures," he said to Salvador, still speaking in Spanish. He had a kind voice. "I see an old man and a dog. It looks almost like this dog. There's a fence, too. A tall fence."

He patted Salvador on the shoulder, and both policemen went to their car. Salvador followed them, catching at their elbows and pointing at the tablet.

"I'm sorry," Delfino said, trying to hold Salvador back. "Just ignore him. I'm sorry."

Arturo spoke to Delfino out the car window. "You need to put that dog on a leash." Then the policemen drove away.

They were city policemen, but they could have turned Delfino and Salvador over to the immigration if they had wanted to. How could Salvador put himself and Delfino in that kind of danger? Except for Teresa, there was nothing for them across the border now that Grandfather had died. There was just their dusty little village with its goat herds and one water well. Delfino had been sad there, and he never wanted to go there again. He wanted to bring Teresa and Melchor here.

He felt a flood of relief that the police hadn't done anything more, but anger quickly followed the relief. Delfino's cheeks were burning. Even Salvador should have known better than to approach a policeman.

" Tlicajquihchihua! How could you do such a stupid thing?" he shouted in Nahuatl. "How could you be so dumb? I'm never going to get anywhere. Not with a deadhead like you always around to mess things up!"

Bandit growled, his eyes fixed on Delfino.

"Be still, Tlashtehqui," Salvador said. Bandit stopped growling, but his neck hair was still ruffled.

"You told me we'd get Uncle José and Lamb." Salvador's normally wooden face was sorrowful. He put the tablet under his arm and walked away, Bandit at his side.

A pain shot through Delfino's heart. He sank to the curb. Drops of water fell onto the pavement between his feet. He touched his cheeks. They were wet.

What's wrong with me? A man doesn't cry.

Then a memory flooded Delfino's mind—a long-buried memory, a memory so vivid he could see nothing else, not the people going in and out of the store, not the scattered empty grocery baskets, not even the many cars. Delfino saw Grandfather and Salvador.

Salvador was about ten years old, and Grandfather had been trying to teach him numbers. Grandfather's face was deeply lined, but it did not wear its familiar gentle expression. Rather, it was frustrated and angry.

Grandfather stood in front of Salvador. He shouted. He raised his arm and struck Salvador across the cheek. Salvador staggered, then stood still, his far-away eyes looking past Grandfather, his expression sorrowful.

Grandfather began to cry. Tears ran down the crevices in his face. He clasped Salvador to him, and held him close, weeping over his shoulder. "Forgive me, my son," Grandfather said. "It is you who must teach me. Maybe it is your *tonali* to teach humility and kindness."

Little Delfino was beside a bush, watching. He saw that Grandfather was in pain.

Then Grandfather saw Delfino, too. "Come here," he said.

Delfino approached slowly, but Grandfather reached out to him and pulled him close. He held both boys in one big hug. "You must love and care for each other," he said. "Always stay close together. Two sticks are harder to break than one."

Delfino never saw Grandfather angry again, and never again heard him speak harshly to Salvador. There were no more formal lessons for Salvador, either, though there were for Delfino. Salvador never learned to add, but he listened to Grandfather's stories, and he learned how to talk to animals.

Grandfather always said, "Salvador has a wise heart. Even the animals know it." Sometimes, though, when Grandfather didn't realize Delfino was watching, Delfino saw him gazing at Salvador, grief marking the deep lines in his face.

Delfino got up from the curb and started to the apartment. He was sick of himself for treating Salvador badly, and he knew that Salvador was right about what they should do. Delfino felt horrible every time he thought of Uncle José at the slave camp. He was a gentle, wise old man like Grandfather had been. Delfino felt bad about the murdered man, too, and about Lamb and the other poor tormented dogs, and about Carlos and Lalo and all the other men, but he longed to live a good life here on this side of the Rio Grande.

Delfino found Salvador and Bandit sitting in the courtyard with Bread Crumb standing between them, a small arm around each of their necks. "Here comes Delfino," he said in his piping voice.

An empty bucket was lying nearby. Delfino picked it up and put it upside down across from Salvador. He sat on it and started to speak, but instead he got up and embraced his cousin. Then he sat down again.

"Salvador, can you forgive me?"

Salvador's eyes lost their vague and distant gaze. For the first time in his life, Delfino saw his cousin look present and aware.

"I forgive you," Salvador said. He did not speak in his familiar flat tone. His voice had expression and resonance.

Delfino was amazed, but in only a moment, Salvador's eyes were distant again. Grandfather used to say, "He sees the place we all came from. The rest of us have forgotten it, but Salvador remembers. Part of him still lives there."

Salvador had returned to his faraway place. Delfino talked to him anyway, as he always had done. "Salvador, you are right. We have to help Uncle José and Lamb. Tonight we will put the pictures you drew in an envelope and mail them to the police. We'll make a map, too. We'll do it together."

And they did. At first, Delfino was just trying to humor his cousin, trying to make up for his harsh words, but as they worked on the map, he began to think it was a good idea. They marked the way they had run in the rain, where the farm with the pond was, Wings and Greens restaurant, and the boxcars at Mexican Hat. Delfino labeled the camp *Lugar de los esclavos de Boss,* Place of Boss's Slaves.

It was past midnight when they finished. Delfino didn't bother Valente this time. He copied the address on the envelope himself. Then Salvador stuck on the stamp, and they walked out in the fresh night air to mail it, Bandit beside them.

Delfino pointed to Bandit, Salvador, and himself. "Like Grandfather used to say, three sticks are harder to break than one." He smiled, remembering how Grandfather used to change the number. If Teresa was with them it was three.

My sister is a frail little stick now, he thought. She's only a slender reed, but Salvador and I are with her. We're strong sticks. We'll send our money. She won't break.

21

Dreams and Disappointments

The next morning, Delfino put on clean clothes, thankful to be going to work for *la señora* Bitsy Clay again. He always tried to be neat, but this morning he took special pains. He tucked his shirt in snugly, combed his hair carefully, and wiped the dust off his shoes. Then he spent time scrubbing his hands and cleaning his nails. Even so, he arrived early at the spot where they were to meet. He expected to find the other workers there early, too, but he was alone.

They've stopped to get *burritos,* he thought. They'll come walking along eating them in just a minute.

But *la señora* Bitsy Clay arrived, and Delfino was still the only one there.

"Oh, I shouldn't have paid them 'til the job was done!" she said. "I never learn. They're drunk someplace. Delfino, do you know someone who can help? The work is too much for you to do alone."

Delfino thought about the men in the apartment. He was sure that some of them could come, but who would be suitable? Everyone seemed too crude to work for *la señora.*

"I'll walk back to the apartment and see who I can find," he said.

"I don't want to wait," *la señora* Bitsy answered impatiently. "Jump in the car, and I'll take you." Everything about *la señora* was quick. Her words, her movements, even the flash of her blue eyes.

As Delfino got in, he noticed a white pickup. He couldn't see the license tag or fender, but he caught a glimpse of the driver. It was a big man in a cowboy hat. Delfino scrunched down in the seat and turned his face away from the window. He felt weak.

It's probably not Boss, he told himself. Houston is full of big men in pickups. But he had to summon his strength to get out at the apartment.

"Un momento," he said.

As he started up the stairs, he bumped into Valente, looking splendid in a new green shirt, boots, and a cowboy hat.

"It's your day off!" Delfino exclaimed. "Boy, am I glad to see you! The other workers didn't show up, and I have to get someone else. Come on. It's a great job."

"Ay de mí," Valente answered good-naturedly as he fell into step with Delfino. "There's no rest when you're around."

Delfino was proud to introduce his handsome, polite friend to *la señora* Bitsy. Later, he was proud of Valente's work, too. He watched him lift an ax over his shoulder, bring it down in a crisp blow, and split a piece of stump neatly in half.

"You swing a mean ax," Delfino said.

"I should. I've carried one on my shoulder enough to be chummy with axes."

"There's something on my mind," Delfino said. "I feel like we are letting Uncle José down. I don't think the police are getting our letters."

"Hombre, they have to get them," Valente answered. "I copied the addresses right, and even if I didn't, the post office knows where the police are."

"Then they aren't paying attention," Delfino said. "They should have found the slave camp by now, but if they had, it would be on the radio. We'd know."

"Maybe you're right. People would have been talking about it." Valente stood still, his hands resting on the ax handle in front of him.

"I think you should telephone the police," Delfino said. "You don't have to tell them who you are. I'd call if I could speak English."

Valente started chopping again.

They worked in silence.

At last Valente said, "Okay, Delfino, I'll do it. I can't think of any way they'd know who I am or where to find me. You should call, too. They'll probably have someone who speaks Spanish."

Delfino hadn't thought of that. He was glad Valente agreed with him. He would feel better after they phoned the police. It was his night to call Teresa, too. He wondered how she was.

He remembered when Teresa and Melchor decided to get married. Padre Ignacio had said they were too young. Melchor had been nineteen and Teresa only fifteen, but Delfino hadn't thought their marriage was a mistake. Melchor was a gentle person, and there weren't many men in Ahuelican who could be called gentle. Delfino had believed that Teresa would be better off to leave their brutal, unhappy home and marry the soft-hearted Melchor. He hadn't thought about Melchor's poverty or his obedience to his conservative parents as being problems then. Now he felt differently.

That afternoon, Bitsy came out to see Delfino's and Valente's work. They had finished splitting the stumps and had filled the holes in with fresh dirt.

"You boys dig and delve like elves!" Bitsy exclaimed. "And you chop like professional woodcutters. You are almost finished!"

Delfino felt a surge of pride. He wasn't used to having his work appreciated.

"Delfino, how would you like to move out here and work for me full time?"

He could hardly believe his ears. To work for someone like *la señora* Bitsy Clay would be a dream come true.

"Señora, I'd like that very much, if my cousin could come, too."

"Oh, no, Delfino. I can only take one person. Isn't your cousin working for Feliciano?"

"Sí, señora, but I can't leave him. Salvador needs me; no one else can speak his language. You could have both of us for the price of one."

"I can't do that, Delfino. I can only take one. You think about it. There is just one more day of work on the trees, and I can't drive into Houston to get you for regular chores. Come on and have a look at the apartment."

Delfino shook his head. He was sick to think his days of working for Bitsy were about to end. Why tease himself by looking?

"Amigo, let's go look," Valente said. He gave Delfino a nudge.

The apartment was over the big garage. It had two small rooms and a bathroom. There was a little cooking stove and a refrigerator. There were dishes, silverware, towels. There was a couch, a chair, and a small television. The bedroom had a chest of drawers, a mirror, and a big bed with a fat mattress. Everything looked clean and new. Delfino had never thought he could have a place like that.

For a moment, he imagined himself sitting casually in the chair, then getting up and going to the refrigerator for a cold drink. He imagined lying in the middle of the big bed, his arms spread out and a smile on his face.

"Tell the lady you'll take it," Valente urged. "I'll keep an eye on Salvador. Bread Crumb's family will, too. You've got friends, *hombre."*

Delfino shook his head again. He couldn't leave Salvador. On the ride into Houston, he struggled to keep from feeling sad, but disappointment covered him like a big dark cloak. He told himself that there must be other easygoing, goofy ladies in Texas who needed workers. But he couldn't quite believe that, so he comforted himself by thinking of the money he had earned.

La señora Bitsy drove straight to the apartment complex. She let Delfino and Valente out. Salvador and Bandit were at the far side of the courtyard. Martin Gonzales was talking to Salvador in rapid Spanish. He was wearing a bright purple shirt, and the sun gleamed on his gold chain.

Salvador shook his head, puzzled.

"Stop playing dumb! You're making money and you have to pay!" Martin Gonzales jabbed his finger into Salvador's chest.

Salvador stepped back. Bandit crouched, ready to leap, but Salvador spoke his name softly, and the dog was still.

Delfino and Valente ran forward. Valente grabbed Martin and jerked him around. The purple shirt tore.

Delfino stood beside Salvador, his fists up and his legs braced. "Don't worry, Cousin," he said in Nahuatl. He was ready to fight, but Valente didn't seem to need any help.

"Who are you calling dumb?" Valente shook his fist in Martin's face. "You're the dumb one! Don't you know that dog could eat you alive!"

"You tore my shirt! You're in real trouble, now. I'll call the *immi.* I'll tell my uncle. He can have you killed."

"Yeah, sure," Valente said. He shoved Martin. "Don't you ever come near my friend again!"

Bandit growled deep in his throat and bared his teeth.

"Tlashtequi! *Chi chi!"*

The dog was still.

"You better pray the *immi* doesn't bother us, you piece of trash. I'll keep some of your pretty clothes so I can give the dog your scent. If we get picked up, you're done for." He tore Martin's shirt off his back. "Get out of here before I smash you with my shoe, you cockroach!"

Delfino had never seen Valente so fierce.

Martin Gonzales's dull features convulsed with hatred. "I'll get you. All of you. You just wait!" He stalked away.

"Ay, Valente," Delfino said. "I knew you were tough, but I didn't know you had a temper like that."

Valente was staring after Martin. "Stupid thug!"

Salvador reached out and clasped Valente's arm gently.

"Come on, Valente," Delfino said. "A shower will help you cool down. Then we'll go eat." He turned to Salvador, "Do you want to come eat with us?"

Salvador shook his head. "We want to take our walk." He turned. "Tlashtequi, come." They walked away together.

Later, when they had showered and were eating enchiladas at the counter in El Mercado, Valente said, "Your cousin and his dog are a strange pair. I don't believe Salvador would even swat a mosquito. But Bandit is ferocious. He's really scary, but he obeys Salvador even when his blood is up."

Delfino nodded. "I don't understand either. I don't think I've ever told you that Aztecs have a god who is a dog." Delfino was half surprised at himself for admitting that.

"Are you kidding? You Aztecs get buried with a red dog, and you pray to one, too?"

"I don't think anyone prays to him. Maybe you remember the story I told you about the warriors killed in battle. They escort the sun from dawn to high noon, and the women who died in childbirth escort the sun in his downward path and put him to bed at night. Well, a god named Xolotl takes the form of a dog and guards the sun until morning."[1]

"I'll drink to that," Valente said, lifting his glass of orange juice. "If old Xolotl is as good a guard as Bandit, I'd say we don't have to waste any worry on the sun."

He and Valente got change for the telephone when they paid for their meals. Delfino went to one phone, Valente to another.

Hands shaking, Delfino dialed the number for the police.

A voice spoke in English. Delfino answered in Spanish. Then he waited.

At last a bored voice said, *"Bueno."*

Words spilled out of Delfino's mouth. He didn't know he would have so much to say. He explained, described, pleaded.

"We'll look into it, sir," the bored voice responded. "Thank you for calling."

"The license tag is BOSS-1," Delfino said. His voice trembled.

"Yes, sir. Thank you for calling."

Delfino hung up, discouraged. He hoped Valente's luck had been better.

"Valente, what did they say? Did they pay attention to you?"

"Maybe. I'm not sure. I had to wait a lot. They kept switching me to different people."

Delfino knew he had to be satisfied with that. Be patient, he told himself, be patient.

Now he could call Teresa. He knew she would be waiting. He looked forward to hearing her light voice, but Melchor answered instead.

"Teresa está muy mala," he told Delfino. "She is very sick. She stays in bed. Now I know that you were right. She needs a doctor. I have to take her to Iguala and find one. I think we have to stay in Iguala until she delivers." There was fear in Melchor's voice. "Doctors are expensive, and to pay for a place to stay in Iguala . . ."

Delfino's whole body went numb. He barely managed to speak. "I'll get money. I'll send it."

There was a place to wire money right there in El Mercado, but all the money he and Salvador had was not enough to pay for Teresa to go to the doctor.

22

Delfino's Wild Ride

The next morning Delfino went out to meet Bitsy carrying his second set of clothes and his tablet. He had lain awake most of the night, trying to think of a solution. He hated to leave Salvador, but there wasn't any other way to help Teresa. Maybe *la señora* Bitsy would even give him his wages in advance, and he could wire money to Mexico that very morning.

Delfino dreaded asking for money he hadn't earned yet. It was humiliating, but he had to do it. He clenched his teeth and stiffened his spine. "*Señora,* I am ready to move to your ranch and work for you full time, but I need some money now."

"That's great, Delfino! I'm glad you changed your mind!" Bitsy's wiry salt-and-pepper hair seemed to vibrate with enthusiasm. Then she exclaimed, "Good heavens! Is that all you have to bring? You are a poor church mouse of a boy. We better go buy you some things while we are in Houston."

"*No, señora*. I don't want clothes. I just want money. I have to send it to my sister now—right now." Delfino was surprised to hear how bold he sounded. He had to hold strong, but he didn't mean to give offense to *la señora* Bitsy.

"Let's go send it then," Bitsy said matter-of-factly. She didn't seem to mind in the least. She put her big purse on her arm, went into El Mercado with him, and filled out the forms. It wasn't hard to send money to Mexico, but Delfino was slow at filling out forms, so he was glad to have Bitsy's help.

Uncle José kept coming into his thoughts. Uncle José limping down the cotton rows . . . lying weakly on his cot . . . calling Salvador one of God's innocents . . . standing at the fence as lightning flashed all around . . .

Delfino wanted to tell *la señora* Bitsy about the camp, but what if she hadn't realized he was illegal? Maybe she hadn't thought about that. If he told her about the camp, she might not hire him after all. What would happen to Teresa then? It was better to keep quiet.

At the ranch, Delfino found his new tasks easy. He learned to use the riding mower. Cutting the grass between the many pine and oak trees and on the flat expanse on one side of the house was pleasant and didn't seem like work at all to him. Even his worries lightened. Teresa and Melchor had gone to Iguala, and the doctor had given Teresa some blood. She was getting stronger. And when he called Salvador at El Mercado, Salvador said he hadn't seen Martin Gonzales since Valente ran him off.

Most days Bitsy got up early and went for a ride on her horse. Delfino liked to see her when she and the horse jumped over bales of hay. But he enjoyed Bitsy in the garden most. She made him laugh. She weeded and watered, wearing baggy shorts and singing off key. She got her knees muddy, and she didn't mind when bees buzzed around her. Her darting movements made her like a bird in her own garden.

He wished Salvador could see the garden. Cardinals chirped their feeding sound. Hummingbirds hovered over all the spots of red. Delfino was sure that if Salvador were there, birds would perch on his shoulders as he worked.

One morning, Bitsy asked Delfino to wash the windows of the house from the outside. "Here," she said. "Play this radio so you won't be bored." But soon, she stuck her head out of the window. There was a smudge of white flour on her sun-browned cheek. "Delfino, do you know how to drive?"

"Nothing but a lawnmower, *señora.*"

"Phooey! I'm out of baking powder. I wanted you to go to the store."

"I can walk, *señora.*" He knew she was thinking of the country store a few miles away.

"Too slow. I'll have to go myself. Rats!"

In a few moments, she zoomed down the driveway.

That evening, people in big cars wearing evening clothes came to visit. Delfino watched out his apartment window as they arrived. Bitsy greeted them, wearing an elegant dress. Her hair was in place, and she had diamonds around her neck.

Pretty fancy, Delfino thought, but I like *la señora* Bitsy better with muddy knees.

The next day Bitsy stopped him as he was starting the lawnmower. "We have something more important to do," she said. "Come on."

They got in an old yellow pickup that was behind the barn. Bitsy took it down the driveway and onto the road.

"Today you learn to drive," she said. "Trade places."

Delfino got out and started around the car. His stomach fluttered, but he tried to look calm.

"Come on!" Bitsy said. "You're slow as molasses."

Delfino slid cautiously behind the wheel. He was so short, he could barely see over it.

Bitsy showed him how to shift the gears. Then she said, "Okay, crank her up."

Delfino looked at her blankly.

"Start it," Bitsy said, "just like you do the lawnmower. Oh—that's the brake."

Delfino turned the key.

"Okay," she said, pointing and gesturing, "push the clutch in, and ease it into first."

The gears made a grinding sound. The pickup jerked and backfired. Delfino felt that he was riding some dreadful monster. He was terrified, but Bitsy seemed perfectly calm.

"Gently," she said. "Just give it gas gently, then push in the clutch and put it in third."

When at last they got rolling smoothly, they rode all around the ranch. They stopped. They started. They backed up. They turned around in the road. They parked. Delfino grinned. He had tamed the monster.

"Time to barrel race!" Bitsy said suddenly. She jumped out and opened the fence gate into the pasture, motioning him to drive in.

Delfino didn't know what was going on. He felt uneasy when Bitsy closed the gate behind him and jumped back in beside him.

"Drive over there, and cut around that barrel!"

That seemed odd, but Delfino put on the gas, then turned the pickup carefully, as close to the barrel as he could.

Maybe she just wants to see if I can turn well, he thought.

"Quick! Head for the next one!" Bitsy shouted. Her blue eyes looked as wild as her salt-and-pepper hair.

Delfino speeded up. His throat tightened.

"Now brake it down! Cut it close!"

Heaven help me! Delfino thought. Aztec or Christian, I don't care. Just help me.

The car careened around the barrel.

"Go around the last barrel! Hit the gas!"

He did—but he didn't make it. He hit the barrel. It went rolling across the pasture, and his heart hit his feet. He stopped the car, ashamed.

But Bitsy was leaning back, laughing with her hands on her stomach.

Delfino started to laugh, too. I could never have imagined working for someone like *la señora* Bitsy, he thought. Not in a million years.

Bitsy was serious, though, almost stern, when she gave him a set of keys to the pickup. "I want you to drive a little every day for practice," she told him, "but you *must not* go into town or get on the highway. Not until you get a license. This is important. Do you promise?"

"Of course, *señora*. Of course."

Then Bitsy was lighthearted again. She walked away singing off key.

Working for her is my good fortune, Delfino thought. But even as he thought about his good luck, he felt a pang for the men toiling down the cotton rows or loading rocks on the slave farm. He was uneasy about Salvador, too. And he still cast fearful glances over his shoulder looking for Boss.

23

The White-Headed Hawk

Bitsy wanted flower beds. Every day Delfino turned a patch of earth with a spade and mixed in rich black earth from plastic bags. One afternoon she sat for a long time in a garden chair gazing toward the work he had done.

"What are you doing, *señora?*"

"I'm thinking of flowers. We are going to plant flowers by the hundreds. Our garden will be a riot of color." She gestured broadly.

"Isn't this Salvador's day off? Let's take the pickup and go into Houston. You can go by and see him for a couple of hours while I get the flowers."

And they were off in the old yellow pickup, the wind blowing in their faces. Delfino was excited. He hadn't seen Salvador for two weeks. When they got to the apartment complex, Salvador and Bandit were sitting in the courtyard.

Bitsy let Delfino out and waved at Salvador. Then she was on her way.

Delfino embraced his cousin. He wanted to take him to a restaurant for supper. There was a little one called Los Alamos not too far from the apartments—just a nice walk away. It was next to the Las Casitas motel.

They strolled happily with Bandit beside them. They chatted only a little. Just to be moving in step together again felt comfortable. When they came to the restaurant, they left Bandit waiting on a grassy area by the motel.

They ate tacos and guacamole salads and ordered a plate for Bandit. All Delfino's worries seemed to have been lifted from his shoulders, and he was at ease. As they left the restaurant, Delfino happened to glance into the motel parking lot. A big white pickup with a red smudge on the fender sat near the street.

Boss has come looking for us, Delfino thought. This motel is the closest one to our apartment. That's why he's here. He's found us. Maybe Martin Gonzales's uncle really did work for Pino. Maybe he had told Boss about them.

Delfino stood between his cousin and the parking lot as Salvador gave Bandit his food. Then he suggested that they walk in a different direction—one that put their backs to the motel lot.

A door slammed. A motor started. At the sound of the motor, Bandit growled.

"Calm yourself, Tlashtehqui," Delfino said in Nahuatl. He knew Bandit had recognized the sound of Boss's pickup. "Calm yourself." Delfino kept moving as he spoke. He didn't so much as glance toward the pickup. He tried not to give the slightest hint that anything was wrong, but Bandit kept growling, and his neck hair stood up. Salvador turned to look. Then Delfino looked, too. The license tag said BOSS-1.

"It's him," Salvador said as the pickup drove away.

"You're right, Cousin. It's Boss."

A hawk circling overhead swooped low and made a sound like laughter. The hawk had a white head. Delfino and Salvador knew that meant danger was near.[1]

Delfino was afraid, but he saw that his cousin was not. There was resignation on Salvador's face—the same stoic resignation and acceptance of fate he had shown in the dog pen facing Slick.

Just as Delfino and Salvador arrived back at the apartment, Bitsy bounced into the parking area. The back of the yellow pickup was a mass of quivering orange-gold blossoms—marigolds. Delfino's heart sank when he saw them. Marigolds were flowers for the dead.[2]

A school bus pulled up at the curb and spilled out a flood of children who scattered in all directions. Bread Crumb was among them. The child came running and hugged Delfino's leg, then Salvador's, and then hugged Bandit. "Now I go to kindergarten," he said proudly.

Salvador picked the little boy up and swung him high so the child could get a good look at the mass of flowers in the pickup. Delfino felt that he was watching from afar. The world seemed unreal. Valente appeared, just returning from work. He approached cheerfully. Delfino clasped the rough, strong reality of his friend's hand, but he himself did not feel like a man of flesh and bone. He was a puppet, and his *tonali* pulled the strings.

"Boss is here," Delfino told Valente, speaking softly. "We saw him. He's at the Las Casitas Motel."

Valente's cheery expression changed, and his jaw set.

Bitsy scratched Bandit under the chin. Then she exclaimed, "My goodness! The finest blossom of all isn't even in the pickup!" And she moved some of the flowers.

"Here is a place for a big flower," she said, gesturing.

"She wants you to put Tzintli in," Delfino told Salvador in Nahuatl.

Salvador placed the child into the empty spot Bitsy had made. Bread Crumb crouched down low and tipped his head back. He wore a big smile. People from the apartments were standing on their porches, watching.

"Isn't this the loveliest flower of all?" Bitsy asked.

Everyone laughed and applauded.

Salvador lifted the child high, and Bitsy gave him a flower. He ran to his mother and gave it to her. They waved and went inside.

"La señora must have many dead to remember," Salvador said, looking at the marigolds. He touched some blossoms gently as he spoke.

Delfino remembered how he and Salvador used to cover Grandfather's grave with marigolds on the Day of the Dead.

Then they would have a simple meal at his graveside. They would talk to Grandfather and tell him all their joys and sorrows.

"On the Day of the Dead, we will scatter marigolds for Grandfather, even though we are here. Grandfather won't mind if we do it here. I'm sure he will hear us anyway," Delfino told Salvador.

As they drove away, Delfino asked, "*Señora*, why did you buy marigolds?" He wondered if *la señora* knew that marigolds were the flowers of the dead. Surely they must have some important meaning to her.

"I got them because it is so hot," Bitsy answered in her matter-of-fact way. "Marigolds don't mind the heat like most flowers do."

Delfino nodded. He saw that *la señora* Bitsy was practical like Valente. They lived in a world without mysteries, not among dreams and signs like he and Salvador did. Delfino had tried to resist the mysteries, but he couldn't. For him and Salvador, omens were real.

The laughter of the white-headed hawk rang in his ears.

24

A Burial Hymn at Dawn

When they got home Bitsy said, "Let's put our flowers in the ground now. That way they can settle during the cool of the night." So Bitsy and Delfino got busy.

They took the marigolds out of their pots, put them in the earth, and gave them a drink.

"Isn't this fun?" she asked. She rubbed her cheek with the back of her hand and left a muddy smudge there.

Delfino nodded. But he wasn't having fun. He was worried. He decided to tell Bitsy about Boss. "*Señora* Bitsy, I have to tell you something." Delfino paused. His throat was so tight it was hard to talk.

"Go ahead," said Bitsy, inspecting a wilted marigold and frowning.

"It is about a bad place, a *rancho* in the country." Delfino struggled on. "I was there before. With many others. It was very hard there. It was too hard, *señora.*"

"I'm sorry to hear that," said Bitsy. She was looking through the marigolds to see if there were other dead flowers. "But things are much better now, aren't they?"

Did she believe he was complaining? Delfino couldn't think how to tell her about the slave camp and breaking rocks and Lamb and Uncle José and Slick and Lázaro and the dogs and the lightning and the cave with the dead man. "The man's name is Boss," he said finally.

A big car came wheeling down the driveway. Bitsy jumped up and ran to meet it. Inside was a man in a pearl gray Stetson and a little girl in a ruffled dress.

In a moment, Bitsy called, "Delfino, I'm quitting now. My cousin is in town, and I'm going to a party. We can talk tomorrow."

She and her visitors went into the house. Before long Delfino saw them leave. He wanted to call out, *Wait . . . wait . . . let me tell you about Boss . . .* but his wooden tongue would not lift to let him speak.

It was dark when Delfino finished. A solid mass of marigolds now bordered the driveway. Delfino climbed the stairs to his apartment, sick with worry and disappointment. Oh, why hadn't he told Bitsy about the slave camp from the first? And why did he let her leave?

He decided to stay up until Bitsy came home. He couldn't wait until tomorrow to tell her. But Delfino was barely able to dry himself after his hot shower before weariness commanded him. He fell into his bed and crossed the border into his old restless dream-troubled sleep.

From afar, Delfino saw himself standing among the flowers of the dead. He had been digging hard and earnestly. Now he picked up armfuls of the golden plants. He was carrying them somewhere, and tears were running down his cheeks as he walked. He told himself not to cry, to accept fate, to be a true Aztec, but the tears would not stop.

He came to the place where he had been digging, and he could see that he had made a grave. He put the marigolds down and looked into the grave.

Salvador lay there. Delfino gazed on his cousin's face. It seemed beautiful to him—noble and good. Bandit lay dead in the grave beside Salvador. Delfino scattered blossoms over both of them.

"I bury you with a red dog, Cousin," Delfino said, "just like the Aztecs of old. Tlashtehqui will guide you across the river and through the hazards of the underworld. He will take you through the clashing rocks and the wind of knives, through the shooting stars and the fiery snakes. You will have a successful journey, but not only because of Tlashtehqui. You will succeed because of what you have already done. You created yourself as an Aztec should. You created your true face. You had the heart of a god."[1]

Delfino covered Salvador and Bandit with earth. Then he covered the grave with marigolds. He kept bringing more and more flowers until the grave was a shimmering golden mound.

In his dream, Delfino saw himself as quite small beside the grave.

Suddenly everything changed.

He was running in a misty, cloudlike land past cages filled with haggard men who stretched their arms toward him and begged for help. Some of the men grabbed his sleeve, but he shook them off and ran away, terrified of the poor wretches.

Then, in the distance, he saw Grandfather. Overjoyed, Delfino ran toward him. Grandfather's face was full of sadness. He shook his head and gazed at Delfino in disappointment. Then he turned his back and walked away.

"Grandfather! Grandfather!" Delfino called.

Grandfather did not answer. He kept walking. He was going toward a distant figure wearing a long poncho that flapped about the knees. Grandfather stretched his arms toward the figure in a loving gesture.

Delfino saw that the person in the poncho was Salvador and that Lamb was in his arms.

Delfino jerked awake. His cheeks were wet. It was almost dawn. He dressed quickly and hurried out of his apartment. He had to tell Bitsy about Boss. And he had to go back to Houston. He had dreamed two death dreams about his cousin. That was a sign—an urgent sign.

Delfino dressed quickly and went outside. The sky was not yet light. He went into Bitsy's screened-in porch and tapped on her back door.

There was no answer.

Delfino knocked louder. And louder.

There was still no answer.

He shouted and banged with all his might, but Bitsy didn't come. Delfino realized that she must have stayed overnight with her relatives. He paced back and forth on the porch. He was frantic with worry.

He wondered if the woman who cleaned for Bitsy might be coming that day. Maybe she would know the phone number of some of Bitsy's relatives. But she might not know. She might not even come today. Delfino had to go see about Salvador. He had to take the pickup.

What if Boss had found Salvador? That wouldn't be hard. A big vague-eyed boy with a big fierce-looking dog was easy to find. Oh, why had he left Salvador alone?

He ran upstairs to his room, got out pencil and paper, and scribbled a note in Spanish. "*Señora,* it's Boss. He will kill Salvador. I had to take the pickup. I'm sorry. Delfino."

He put the note in the back screen door. Then he started the yellow pickup and was off. He wanted to go as fast as the pickup would take him, but he was afraid to go over the speed limit. If he did, he might be stopped for speeding. They might even think he had stolen the truck. It seemed to him that he was crawling down the highway. He tensed his muscles as if he could help by pushing.

Oh, Salvador, be alive. Be alive.

The sky was brightening with dawn light. Suddenly Delfino found himself remembering a long forgotten chant—a burial hymn Grandfather had taught him. He began to sing.

Awaken, already the dawn has come,
already the flame-colored pheasants are singing,
already the fire-colored swallows flutter,
already butterflies are on the wing.
Awaken, the sky is tinged with red.

Why am I singing this? Salvador isn't dead. He can't be. I couldn't bear it. My dreams made me sorrowful. That's the reason I am singing this mournful song. Salvador has the heart of a god, and I don't. I know I have disappointed Grandfather. My sadness has to be because of that. It's not because Salvador is dead—oh, please, not because my cousin is dead.

The song would not leave his lips—it kept rising from his heart, a plaintive Aztec cry.

25

A Knife-Tongued Coyote and a Ship of Gold

When Delfino got to the apartment complex, he parked quickly, leaped out of the pickup, and ran across the courtyard.

Salvador can't die, he thought as he ran. That can't happen. I can't let it.

He ran up the stairs two at a time and burst into the apartment, calling, "Salvador! Salva—!"

Fear killed the sound on Delfino's lips.

Boss was there. He was holding Bread Crumb. Delfino saw the child's lip quiver.

Delfino rushed toward the little boy. Then he stopped short.

Boss had a gun.

Delfino's heart pounded as never before. He was afraid that Bread Crumb might cry or struggle. Bread Crumb's wide brown eyes were fixed on him. Delfino lifted his hand slightly—a signal for Bread Crumb to remain still. The little boy's expression showed that he understood. Only then did Delfino look around the room.

Valente, Salvador, and Bandit stood side by side. Valente's fists were clenched, ready for the first chance to fight. Salvador, with Bandit beside him, gazed toward Boss. His vague eyes gave no clue to his thoughts.

"Well, well," Boss said to Delfino in Spanish. "It looks like the last maverick straggled in all by himself. Saves me a heap of trouble."

The sound of Boss's raspy voice was horrible, and Bread Crumb's face was terrified.

"Let the child go," Delfino said.

Boss smiled. It wasn't a pleasant sight. He chuckled, and a lump of tobacco moved in his cheek. "Can't do that," he said. "This little bit of small change is a good guide. He led me right in. Now we're going to take a little ride." Boss gestured toward Valente. "Smart Stuff can lead the way. You and the simpleton can follow him single file."

Outside the sun hid its face in a cloud. The room darkened. Delfino moved toward Salvador and Valente. Could they jump Boss and snatch the gun?

Boss must have guessed Delfino's thoughts. "If a single one of you peons steps out of line, I drop this kid in a trash bin, and he won't never climb out."

Delfino knew he must not try to get the gun. He couldn't take the chance. Not with Bread Crumb in danger.

The apartment door swung open.

Bitsy Clay stood in the doorway in her denim shorts with her big purse on her arm.

"Señora!" Delfino gasped.

Boss looked surprised. Then he grinned. A skinny little old lady wasn't anything but an amusement to him.

For one moment Delfino was glad to see Bitsy. Then he was sorry he had left the note that brought her into danger. She was smart, and she was spunky, but Delfino knew she wasn't a match for Boss. *La señora* couldn't know what she was up against, and she couldn't see Boss's gun. He had it hidden behind Bread Crumb, and the apartment was dim.

"Señora! Boss has a gun. He'll shoot Bread Crumb."

Bitsy's hand reached into her purse.

"He's a killer," Delfino said, talking fast. "We used to be slaves on his farm, then we broke out . . ."

"Ma'am, you don't want to take these Mezcan kids too seriously."

Bitsy's eyes flashed. "I'd make lard out of you just for saying that if I didn't already have a better reason," she said. She sounded like she could stand toe to toe with the devil and stare him down.

But what about Bread Crumb? Delfino could barely breathe, he was so afraid.

Suddenly the sun lifted its face from the clouds and shone through the window. Everything changed at that moment. Golden light streamed in. Light reflected off Bandit's thick red coat. He seemed to be outlined in gold. A power from the ancient past moved before Delfino's eyes.

Delfino looked toward Salvador and saw the face of an Aztec warrior—not awaiting death but strong for life. He nodded at his cousin.

Salvador spoke. "Tlashtehqui!"

Bandit understood. Before Boss could move, he leaped forward, a flash of red power. *Tonali* was at work. Tlashtehqui's smooth coat grew rough, and his fierce eyes glowed yellow as the sun. He became a huge coyote, knife-tongued, vengeful.[1] Snarling, he struck Boss on the chest.

Bread Crumb broke free.

Fear filled Boss's eyes as he fell, Tlashtehqui's fangs at his throat. He dropped the gun. It fired. The bullet whizzed by Salvador's head. He didn't flinch.

"*Chi chi!*" Salvador commanded. Bandit froze, his fangs still at Boss's fat throat.

Valente grabbed the fallen gun and pointed it at Boss.

Bitsy pointed a gun at Boss, too. Her graying hair was standing up crazily. Even now, she made Delfino smile. He wondered what else she might have in her bottomless purse.

Bread Crumb started kicking Boss. "You lied. You told me you had money for Salvador," he shouted. "And my name's not Small Change. My name is Bread Crumb. It's Tzintli! Tlashcaltzintli!"

There was the sound of running feet. Two men, a young one and an older one, in identical Western clothes dashed into the room, guns drawn. "Texas Rangers!" they shouted. "Drop your weapons."[2]

"Tlashtehqui!"

Bandit went to Salvador. Bread Crumb followed, and Salvador rested his hand on the child's head.

The Rangers took the guns and put Boss under arrest.

"You doin' all this for a couple of Mezcan kids?" Boss asked as the younger Ranger handcuffed him.

"For them, and a few others," the older one answered. "For the ones penned up on your spread down South where you think you're a new Duke,[3] and for some other meanness you've been into."

"You're mighty interested in Pino, ain't you, Captain?" Boss was speaking to the older Ranger. "I can tell you all about his operation and where he is. We can do a little horse trading, can't we? Lemme go and I'll take you to him."

"Pino's already as good as caught," the Captain answered.

Boss spit a brown stream on the floor as the younger Ranger led him away.

"Well now. That's done," Bitsy said cheerfully. "Come on, Bread Crumb. We're going to take you home before we go downtown."

Later, at the police station, there were a lot of questions. When they finished answering, Ranger Captain McCullough said, "Sure appreciate your making that call, Ma'am."

La señora called the Rangers when she read my note, Delfino realized with a surge of pride.

"Did you already know about Boss, Captain McCullough?" Bitsy asked.

"Partly, Ma'am. A man named Buck Sams had his suspicions. Then a preacher down near Mexican Hat tipped us off. He heard about the camp from a fellow in his congregation named Washington."

"The Houston police began getting letters and phone calls, too," the younger Ranger, Bud Liner, added. "Finally they even got a hand drawn map. The farm and all was a cover for Boss's drug running."

Salvador's map! It had worked!

"Your phone call told us where we could pick Boss up, but a few Rangers had already gone down to that slave camp. Actually, they might have it cleaned out by now. Let's see." Captain McCullough dialed the phone. He talked for a few minutes; then he smiled broadly and handed the phone to Delfino.

Delfino and Valente both got to speak to Uncle José. Lamb was still alive and Uncle José was taking him back to his daughter's house. Buck Sams was going to find homes for the other dogs.

Delfino was glad about all that, and he tried to keep his voice from quivering as he said, *"Señora,* you are a magnificent and funny lady. I am sorry we are going to have to leave you. Now they will send us back to Mexico."

Bitsy looked at Captain McCullough. Delfino followed her gaze. Sunlight struck the Captain's badge. Delfino looked at it closely. "Ay, *Capitán!* I saw a dead man with a badge like that. He was shot through the head."

"You found a dead man wearing a Ranger badge?"

"Yes, *Capitán.* A skeleton. I fell in a cave in Boss's hills and found him."

"I understand Kent Oliver's been missing ten years now," Ranger Bud Liner said. "That drug case has never been solved."

"I bet my bottom dollar that's him," Captain McCullough said. "Boss must have been the drug runner Oliver was tracking. I never did believe he ran off to Mexico with the loot like folks said."

"Wouldn't there be a reward for turning in Oliver's killer?" Bitsy asked.

"Yes, ma'am. If that's Oliver, these boys won't have any money worries for quite a spell."

Valente grinned broadly as he translated.

Delfino drew a deep breath. There would be money for Teresa.

"Well, catching a big crook and finding a missing Ranger should merit a green card, too," Bitsy put in. "Right, Captain?"

"Ma'am, it just might. We'll see what we can do. Are you going to take the boys with you?"

"Of course," Bitsy said cheerfully, "I can't imagine how I ever thought one boy could do all the work I have to do. I definitely need three boys and a dog."

As they left, Valente said, *"Señora,* I don't want to seem ungrateful, but I have to go back to Monterrey for school soon. Maybe Delfino could invite me to come visit next summer if he wants to keep in touch."

"Are you kidding? Like you once said, you are stuck with me forever," Delfino answered, putting his arm around Valente's shoulder.

"Let's get going," Bitsy said in her familiar hasty way. "We might as well buy some more marigolds while I have plenty of workers."

She got in her car, and Delfino followed in the pickup. Valente sat beside him. Salvador and Bandit rode in the back. Bitsy led them to a store where there were thousands of plants, and they filled the pickup with golden marigolds.

The dream warned me, but we kept it from coming true, Delfino thought. These marigolds aren't for Salvador's grave. In this country, they aren't for graves at all.

"Don't you and Bandit want to ride with me?" Bitsy asked Salvador.

But Salvador wanted to ride outside, so they pushed the flowers closer together until he and Bandit could just fit inside the tailgate. Then they were off, Bitsy leading in her Cadillac.

Delfino's heart sang. Once more, he could see himself as through an eagle's eye. He was streaming down the highway in a yellow pickup loaded with one friend, one dog, one cousin, and countless blossoms. It was his ship of gold sailing the promised land.

Notes

Chapter 1: The Crossing

1. *Coyote* is a slang term for the person who leads Mexicans across the border illegally. The word is used by English and Spanish speakers alike and is pronounced with the accent on the second of the three syllables.

2. Lady Precious Green and the heaven for the drowned:

> A special resting place called Tlalocán was reserved for those who had died by drowning or of diseases associated with water, such as dropsy. It was the home of the rain god and his consort Chalchihuitlicue . . . whose name can be translated Lady Precious Green. In this heaven the spirits disported themselves, happily playing and constantly singing the praises of the gods in a world which was full of green vegetation, butterflies, and a constant thin rain which reflected rainbows in all directions. To the dwellers on the arid plateau of Mexico, this was a concept of extreme happiness. Thus for those who had died naturally through the waters, there was a place of beauty and joy. There was probably some inner connection with fertility rituals in this belief, but it is not explicit in any of the surviving documents (Burland 30).

3. The moon was thought of in two ways. One was as Lady Golden Bells, Coyolxauhqui, the sister of Huitzilopochtli. The other, perhaps more magical, was as the goddess Tlazolteotl, who in her third phase would absorb the evils perpetrated by mankind and purify the soul. Alas, the name of this purifying goddess translates "the Eater of Filth" (Burland 36).

4. The Aztecs thought each person was born with his special fate, or *tonali*. However, a person's actions could alter his fate for better or for worse (Fagan 222). The individual has the responsibility for creating his own "face" and heart.

Chapter 2: The Promised Land

1. The Virgin of Guadalupe:

> One of the best-known apparitions of the Blessed Virgin, occurring four times at Guadalupe, Mexico, in 1531. Our Lady appeared for the first time to the Indian Juan Diego (declared Blessed in 1990) on December 12, 1531, at Tepeyac, a hill just outside of Mexico City. The Virgin instructed him to go to the local bishop, Juan de Zumárraga, and inform him that she desired a church to be built on the site where she had been seen. The bishop was at first reluctant to believe the earnest visitor, asking for some kind of sign. When the Virgin heard about the bishop's request, she instructed Juan Diego to go and gather roses, even though it was not the season for them. Obediently, he went to the place as told and there found the roses. Gathering them into his cloak (called a tilma by the Indians), he returned to the Virgin, who commanded him to go back to the bishop, instructing him not to open the cloak until he reached his destination. Once more before the bishop, Juan Diego unfolded the cloak. The roses fell out, but even more amazing was the life-size depiction of the Virgin, exactly as Juan Diego had described her, imprinted upon the tilma.
>
> Under Zumárraga's leadership, a church was erected, and the tilma soon became an object of great veneration among the Native Americans in Mexico. . . . The tilma is today preserved in the Basilica of Our Lady of Guadalupe. . . . The Virgin is depicted with the sun, moon, and stars, and an angel beneath the crescent moon. . . . (Bunson 386)

The Hill of Tepeyacac was once a shrine of the mother of Huitzilopochtli. And the radiant apparation spoke in Nahuatl. (Fagan 294)

The many Mexicans, both male and female, named Guadalupe, or Lupe for short, are named for this virgin. December 12 is the Feast Day of our Lady of Guadalupe. December 9 is Juan Diego's Feast Day.

2. Quetzalcoatl and the morning offering: Quetzalcoatl was . . . "the god whose name is often translated as Feathered Serpent, and who demanded no sacrifice except fruit and flowers" (Burland 18–21).

> It was the custom to cut one's ears with a cactus spine and take two drops of blood on two fingers which were then lifted up to cast the blood in the direction of the Morning Star. This was a little offering of discomfort and life's substance, meant to please the god Quetzalcoatl (Burland 36).

Venus, or the Morning Star, was the symbol of Quetzalcoatl.

3. Quetzalcoatl:

> . . . was sent by the supreme god to be an earthly king. This god-king went through a career as a good ruler, but fell victim to temptation by the witch goddess. He was intoxicated by her [magic herbs]. When he recovered he realized that he had broken the sacred traditions and must leave Mexico, taking with him his dwarfs, and other creatures, who all eventually died on the journey. . . . The Toltecs, and all later peoples, remained sure that Quetzalcoatl was fated to return. The power behind the witch goddess . . . Huitzilopochtli, known both as Blue Hummingbird and as Smoking Mirror, was to become the patron of the Aztecs. This power demanded bloody sacrifices (Burland 14).

Thus, from the earliest days, there was a god of peace and a god of violence.

Chapter 3: A Free Ride

1. Butterflies and the happy dead:

> . . . There were occasional visits from the happy dead, who came to reassure their relatives that all was well. These souls appeared, most charmingly, as beautiful butterflies which came and flew around the house, and especially around the bouquets of flowers which were normally carried by Aztec men of any social rank. It was considered ill-mannered to smell a bouquet of flowers from the top: it should always be sniffed at the side, for the top was left for the souls to visit, where they could enjoy the fragrance thus reserved especially for them (Burland 32).

2. The short, fat dog in the dream sequence is modeled on the red clay dogs from Colima which date from the fourth and fifth centuries A.D. They were found in tombs. The wolflike animal it becomes is modeled on the rough and hungry-looking dogs painted by David Alfaro Siqueiros (1896–1974) and from the knife-tongued coyote on Montezuma's sword. (Sword is pictured in Dickey 158.)

Chapter 4: The Farm

1. Contemporary slave camps: In the 1990s, there have been several incidents of illegal immigrants being held in forced labor. In both New York and California, there were prominent incidents in the garment industry. In 1990, near Los Angeles, a group of men were kept behind a seven-foot fence. One of the men, Maldonado, said, "We found ourselves in the mouth of the wolf."

Chapter 6: Enemies and Friends

1. On the third day after death the soul started its journey with a red dog for company. There were several terrible ordeals

to be faced. One was the wind of knives, "where sharp blades of flint had cut all the flesh from their bones. This part of the underworld was populated by living skeletons who held ceremonies and feasts around the court of the great Lord of the Dead" (Burland 29).

Chapter 7: A Dog Named Bandit, a Friend Named Valente

1. Grandfather's speech likening moderation to walking along a peak is from the sixth book of Fray Bernardino de Sahagun's Florentine Codes: *General History of the Things of New Spain* (written in 1569). Grandfather's words are a quotation that Sahagun records of an Aztec nobleman addressing his son (Fagan 139).

Chapter 8: Salvador Risks All

1. Salvador's acceptance of fate: Bernal Diaz noted the Aztec warrior's "terrible forgetfulness of self." In the last battle for Tenochtitlan, the warriors ignored the swords pointed at them and pushed forward. They forgot themselves as individuals. "The warrior in mortal action was freed from the constraints placed on humans in this world . . ." and was "transformed by the fact of his capture into predestined victim." The last moments of the warrior who accepted his death had a transcendental quality. His destiny was revealed, and he embraced it (Clendinnen 150).

2. Being buried with a red dog: "At death, providing it was through natural causes, the body was dressed up in fine clothes, a red dog was slaughtered to accompany it on the journey" (Burland 29). Actually, cremation seems to have been used more often than burial.

Chapter 10: Devil Mountains and Devil Work

1. Mictlan:

The dreary underworld of Mictlan lay beneath the steppes of the north. It was cold and dim. Mictlantecuhtli and his wife Mictecaciuatl ruled over this land. His face was covered with a bony mask, and owls and spiders were around him (Soustelle 107).

2. Quetzalcoatl's temptation:

As the boy grew up, evil magicians tried to tempt him to perform human sacrifices, but he would have none of this, being so filled with love toward all living things that he could not even be persuaded to kill a forest bear or to pick a flower (Nicholson 88).

Chapter 11: The Bones of the Dead

1. Tlaloc:

Tlaloc is a rain god. He brings rain of all qualities. The northern rains were destructive. Indeed, only that of the east is good. Tlaloc lives in the mountains with his dwarfs and with the maize goddesses. When the dwarfs smash their jars, there is thunder; falling pieces of the jars are thunderbolts. There were many Tlaloque. Every mountain had its Tlaloc (Alexander 71).

Chapter 13: Paradise Found

1. The Day of the Dead is widely celebrated in Mexico on November 2. Marigolds are used for this day only and at no other time. Altars are made and strewn with marigolds. Pictures of dead loved ones are placed on the altar along with objects that person was attached to and with favorite foods.

This day is celebrated with an evening meal to which all the souls of all the departed members of the family are invited.

They are told news of the family and the hopes that the parents hold for the next generation, and they are asked to pray for them in the heaven to which they will return the following morning (Burland 41).

The village of Mixquic was a place of contact with the Aztec underworld. Today it is famous for its Day of the Dead celebration. The townspeople cover their relatives' graves with marigolds and fill the cemetery with the smoke of candles and incense. A platform of skulls and bones holds flowers, candles, and fruit.

In markets children buy sugar skulls with their names traced in icing, or a chocolate coffin with a toy skeleton inside. The skeletons are humorous, to show that death is nothing to be feared. It is another phase of our lives, nothing more (Stuart 189).

2. *Cenotes* are deep limestone pools.

The sacred well at Chichén Itzá is surrounded by vertical cliffs sixty-five feet high and offerings were thrown into the water. Originally these were simple votive offerings of clay and rubber; later ceremonies were elaborate, with offerings of gold and jewels (Nicholson 19).

There is a pyramid dedicated to Quetzalcoatl at Chichén Itzá.

Chapter 14: Wings and Greens

1. The legend about the women who died in childbirth putting the sun to bed each night may be found in Burland 31–32.

Chapter 15: A Beating Heart

1. Illegals often die in boxcars. There was an incident like this a few years ago in South Texas. The boxcars were being treated with pesticide, and everyone trapped inside died.

2. Night Axe: Dreams were very important to the Aztecs and priests devoted themselves to interpreting them. Unfortunately, Sahagun did not consider them important and did not record many. However, he did record the "terrible phantom, Night Axe—a headless torso scuttling along the ground, its split chest opening, then shutting with the dull 'chunk' of an axe blow" (Clendinnen 146).

3. Picking a hole in the boxcar: This is an accurate portrayal of how some illegals arrive and how they get out of the boxcar.

Chapter 18: A Little Crumb

1. The story of Tata and Nena is one of the Aztec creation legends (Nicholson 53–54).

Chapter 19: The Remarkable Bitsy Clay

1. To move sedately was an Aztec virtue. "Do not throw thy feet much, nor raise thy feet high . . . lest thou be named fool, shameless . . . Nor art thou to go trampling; thou art not to seem like a firefly, not to strut, not to bustle about . . ." Fray Bernardino de Sahagun gives this quotation in his *General History* (Fagan 139).

Chapter 21: Dreams and Disappointments

1. The legend about a god named Xolotl who takes the form of a dog and guards the sun through the night may be found in Dickey 155 .

Chapter 23: The White-Headed Hawk

1. White-headed hawk:

> When Aztec merchants, traveling far roads, heard the laughter of the white-headed hawk, they knew that danger was waiting. It was the leader's charge to steady his men, not, we are told, by denying the omen, but by yielding to its implications. He was to remind them that their kin had lamented when the merchant train departed, pouring out "their sorrow, their weeping, that perhaps here, somewhere, on the desert, on the plain, in the gorge, in the forest, will lie scattered our bones and our hair, in many places our blood, our redness, will spread, poured out and slippery." Should that moment come, "let no one feel womanish in heart. Yield completely to death . . ." (Clendinnen 151)

Houston is in the Gulf Coastal Plain of Texas. There are many trees, vegetation is lush, and there is abundant bird life. The projected building of an airport had to be canceled because of the threat to nesting cranes. Although hawks are not the most common of birds in Houston, they do appear. A Red-tailed Hawk landed in the author's back yard as this book was being written. The hawk that Delfino sees is probably either a Mississippi Kite or a male Northern Harrier. Interestingly, the call of the Northern Harrier is "a rapid, nasal chattering *ke ke ke ke ke*" like the sound of laughter (*Audubon Society Master Guide to Birding,* Vol 1 226).

2. Marigolds were the particular flowers of the goddess, Xochiquetzal. She was a particularly beautiful lady, and her name means beautiful flowers—*xochitl* meant flower, and *quetzal* meant precious or beautiful. She was the goddess of flowers, of happiness, and of lovemaking. She was also the guardian of graves. Graves are strewn with marigolds on the Day of the Dead (Burland 41).

Chapter 24: A Burial Hymn at Dawn

1. When Delfino says Salvador has the heart of a god, he is alluding to the Aztec belief that they were born with a physical heart and face, but they had to "create a deified heart and a true face." Heart-making and face-making represented the development of spiritual strength. This was "the aim of life" (Nicholson 74).

Chapter 25: A Knife-Tongued Coyote and a Ship of Gold

1. The big coyote with a knife-tongue is portrayed on Montezuma's beautiful ceremonial featherwork shield which he inherited from the Emperor Ahuizotl, the ruler before the succession of Montezumas. The large knife-tongued coyote was Emperor Ahuizotl's symbol. The shield is in the Museum für Völkerkunde, Vienna.

2. The Texas Rangers were the chief law-enforcement body of Texas for more than a hundred years—until 1935. They are now combined with the Department of Public Safety, but are an elite group comprising the most decorated highway patrol officers. Their focus is chiefly on detective work. The ranks in the Rangers are: Sergeant, Lieutenant, Captain (there are six captains in the state), Assistant Commander, and Commander.

3. The word *duke* rather than *king* or *emperor* is used as a reference to power because it is a Texas allusion to a notorious powerhouse from South Texas—George Parr was known as the Duke of Duval (1901–1975). At his peak, the Duke's power extended over fifteen counties.

In the 1950s, he was accused of maintaining a private army of *pistoleros* at taxpayer expense. He was also accused of tax evasion, theft, and of stealing money from the Benivedes School District. Ultimately in 1973, he was convicted of income tax evasion and was sentenced to ten years in prison, five of which were suspended, and he was fined $14,000. He committed suicide in 1975.

The Duke of Duval had charge of Jim Wells County when Lyndon Baines Johnson ran for the senate against Coke Stevenson. That was the election in which the box from Precinct 13 is said to have been stuffed. The voting list mysteriously disappeared, and LBJ won the election. It was because of this election that LBJ got the name "Landslide Lyndon."

Pronunciation Guide to Nahuatl (Aztec) Words

Ahuelican—Ah - way - lee - **cahn**

Chalchihuitlicue—Chal - chee - weet - **lee** - kway

Coatlicue—Co - aht - **lee** - kway

Coatzintli—**Co** - ah - tseent - lee

Mictlan—**Meek** - tlahn

Mictlantecuhtli—**Meek** - tlahn - teh - **coot** - lee

Nahuatl—**Nah** - wahtl

Quetzalcoatl—Keht - zahl- **co** - atl

Tlaloc—**Tlah** - lohk

Tlashcaltzintli—Tlahsh - cahl - **tseent** - lee

Tlashtehqui—Tlahsh - **teh** - kee

Tlicajquihchihua—Tlee - kai - kee - **chee** - wah

tonali—toh - **nah** - lee

Tzintli—**Tseent** - lee

Xolotl—**Shoh** - lohtl

Ychcaconetl—Eech - kah - coh - **nehtl**

Chapter Opening Art

Frontispiece A statue of a snake like this may be seen in the Museo Nacional de Antropología, Mexico City, Mexico.

1 **The Crossing** Chalchihuitlicue, Lady Precious Green, whirlpool manifestation. A featherwork representation of this goddess may be found in the Museo Nacional de Antropología, Mexico City, Mexico.

2 **The Promised Land** Quetzalcoatl. A statue of this god may be found in the British Museum, London, England.

3 **A Free Ride** Colima dog. Pottery figures of these dogs are widespread. One is in the Museum of Fine Arts, Houston, Texas.

4 **The Farm** Coatlique, a goddess representative of the fertility of the earth. A statue of this goddess may be found in the Museo Nacional de Antropología, Mexico City.

5 **Dogs from Hell** Artist's interpretation.

6 **Enemies and Friends** Feathered Serpent and Smoking Mirror. Statues of these lords of life and death may be seen at the Brooklyn Museum, New York.

7 **A Dog Named Bandit, a Friend Named Valente** Eagle warrior. This head may be seen at the Museo Nacional de Antropología, Mexico City.

8 **Salvador Risks All** Aztec Standard Bearer. A statue of a standard bearer may be seen at the Museum of Fine Arts, Houston, Texas.

9 **Eavesdropping and Spying** Xolotl. A statue of this god in his human shape may be seen in the Museum für Völkerkunde, Berlin, Germany.

10 **Devil Mountains and Devil Work** Mictlantecuhtli, Lord of the Dead. A statue of this god may be seen in the Museo Nacional de Antropología, Mexico City.

11 **The Bones of the Dead** Skull rack. A skull rack may be seen in the Museo Nacional de Antropología, Mexico City.

12 **Free at Last** The Evening Star at the crossroads of fate. Codey Fejervary-Mayer, Liverpool City Museum, Liverpool.

13 **Paradise Found** Woman Who Escorts the Sun. A statue of this god may be seen in the Museo de Antropología, Universidad Veracruzana, Jalapa.

14 **Wings and Greens** Olmec head. An Olmec head may be seen in the Museo de Antropología, Universidad Veracruzana, Jalapa, Mexico.

15 **A Beating Heart** Night Axe. A "terrible phantom" that appeared in dreams, "a headless torso scuttling along the ground, its split chest opening, then shutting with the dull 'chunk' of an axe blow" (Clendinnen 146).

16 **Delfino's First Dollar** Dancer. A dancer statue may be seen in the Museo Nacional de Antropología, Mexico City.

17 **A Swarm of Bees** Xipe Totec, from a tomb at Monte Alban.

18 **A Little Crumb** Priest of the Fire God. A statue of this priest may be found in the Museum of the American Indian, New York.

19 **The Remarkable Bitsy Clay** Xochiquetzal, the Flower Goddess. A statue of this goddess may be seen in the Museum für Völkerkunde und Schweizerisches Museum für Volkskunde Basel, Basel, Switzerland.

20 **Grandfather Remembered** Tonacatecuhtli, Lord of Fate. A statue of this god may be seen in the Museum für Völkerkunde und Schweizerisches Museum für Volkskunde Basel, Basel, Switzerland.

21 **Dreams and Disappointments** Xolotl, the dog deity. A statue of this deity may be seen in the Museum für Völkerkunde, Vienna.

22 **Delfino's Wild Ride** A snake. A statue of a laughing snake may be seen in the Museum of Mankind, London, England.

23 **The White-Headed Hawk** Ehecatl, the God of Wind. A representation of this god may be seen in the Codex Borbonicus at the Bibliotheque du Palais-Bourbon, Paris.

24 **A Burial Hymn at Dawn** Xochipilli, the Lord of the Flowers. A statue of this god may be seen in the Museo Nacional de Antropología, Mexico City, Mexico.

25 **A Knife-Tongued Coyote and a Ship of Gold** A feather shield representation of the knife-tongued coyote may be seen in the Museum für Völkerkunde, Vienna, Austria.

Works Consulted

Alcina Franch, José. *Códices mexicanos*. Madrid: Mapfre, 1992.

Alexander, Hartley Burr. *Latin American Mythology*. New York: Cooper Square, 1964.

Berdan, Frances F. *The Aztecs of Central Mexico*. New York: Holt, Rinehart and Winston, 1982.

Burland, C. A. and Werner Forman. *The Feathered Serpent and the Smoking Mirror*. New York: Putnam, 1975.

Bierhorst, John, translator. *History and Mythology of the Aztecs: The Codex Chimalpopoca*. Tucson: University of Arizona Press, 1992.

Boone, Elizabeth Hill. *The Codex Magliabechiano and the Lost Prototype of the Magliabechiano Group*. Berkeley: University of California Press, 1983.

Bunson, Matthew. *Our Sunday Visitor's Encyclopedia of Catholic History*. Huntington, Indiana: Our Sunday Visitor Publishing Division, 1995.

Campbell, Joseph. *The Power of Myth*. New York: Doubleday, 1988.

———. *The Way of the Seeded Earth: Mythologies of the Primitive Planters: The Middle and Southern Americas*. New York: Harper & Row, 1989.

———. *The Way of the Seeded Earth: The Sacrifice*. New York: Harper & Row, 1989.

Clendinnen, Inga. *Aztecs*. New York: Cambridge University Press, 1991.

Dibble, Charles E. *Codex in Cruz Atlas*. Salt Lake City: University of Utah Press, 1981.

Dickey, Thomas, Vance Muse, and Henry Wiencek. *The God-Kings of Mexico*. Chicago: Stonehenge Press, 1982.

Dunham, Lowell. *The Aztecs: People of the Sun.* Norman: University of Oklahoma Press, 1958.

Fagan, Brian M. *The Aztecs.* New York: W.H. Freeman, 1984.

Farrand, John, Jr., ed. *The Audubon Society Master Guide to Birding.* New York: Alfred A. Knopf, 1983.

Gruzinski, Serge. *Man-Gods in the Mexican Highlands: Indian Power and Colonial Society, 1520–1800.* Translated from the French by Eileen Corrigan. Stanford, CA: Stanford University Press, 1989.

Nicholson, Irene. *Mexican and Central American Mythology.* New York: Peter Bedrick, 1985.

Portillo, Miguel León. *Aztec Thought and Culture.* Translated from the Spanish by Grace Lobanov and Miguel León Portillo. Norman: University of Oklahoma Press, 1963.

———. *Pre-Columbian Literatures of Mexico.* Translated from the Spanish by Grace Lobanov and Miguel León Portillo. Norman: University of Oklahoma Press, 1969.

Soustelle, Jacques. *The Daily Life of the Aztecs.* Translated from the French by Patrick O'Brien. New York: MacMillan, 1962.

———. *The Four Suns.* Translated from the French by Patrick O'Brien. New York: Grossman Publishers, 1971.

Sten, María. *Las extraordinarias historias de los códices mexicanos.* Tabasco, Mexico: Joaquín Mortíz, 1972.

Stuart, Gene S. *The Mighty Aztecs.* Washington, D.C.: National Geographic Society, 1981.

Thompson, Eric. *Mexico before Cortez.* New York: Charles Scribner's Sons, 1933.

Vaillant, George C. *Aztecs of Mexico.* New York: Doubleday, Doran & Co.,1941.

Vázquez, Germán. *Origen de los mexicanos.* Madrid: Hermanos García Noblejas, 1987.

Waters, Frank. *Mexico Mystique.* Chicago: Swallow Press, 1975.

Weaver, Muriel Porter. *The Aztecs, Maya, and Their Predecessors: Archeology of Mexoamerica.* 2nd ed. New York: Academic, 1981.